Cairo Modern

Cairo Modern

Naguib Mahfouz

Translated by
William M. Hutchins

The American University in Cairo Press
Cairo   New York

First published in 2008 by
The American University in Cairo Press
113 Sharia Kasr el Aini, Cairo, Egypt
420 Fifth Avenue, New York, NY 10018
www.aucpress.com

Dar el Kutub No. 20274/07
ISBN 978 977 416 156 8

Dar el Kutub Cataloging-in-Publication Data

Mahfouz, Naguib, 1911–2006
        Cairo Modern / Naguib Mahfouz; translated by William M.
   Hutchins.—Cairo: The American University in Cairo Press, 2008
        p.   cm.
        ISBN 977 416 156 4
        1. Arabic fiction   I. Hutchins, William M. (trans.)   II. Title
        813

1 2 3 4 5 6 7 8   12 11 10 09 08

Designed by Andrea El-Akshar
Printed in Egypt

1

he sun had begun a slow descent from its heavenly apogee, and over the university's magnificent dome its disc appeared to be bursting into the sky or returning from its rounds. It flooded treetops, verdant earth, silver-walled buildings, and the great avenue running through the Orman Gardens with rays gentled by frigid January, which had tempered their flame and infused them with benign compassion. Standing at the head of two rows of lofty trees lining the avenue, the dome resembled a god before whom worshipful priests kneel for afternoon prayer. The sky was clear except for some thin, far-flung clouds at the horizon. A chill breeze shook the trees, and their leaves responded with moans and sighs.

Bewildered kites circled overhead and down below—engrossed in separate discussions—groups of students walked along, spilling from the university campus onto the avenue. Then, in the midst of these young men, appeared a group of no more than five female students who advanced diffidently, exchanging confidences. The presence of women at the university was still a novelty that evoked interest and curiosity, especially among the first-year students, who began to exchange glances as they whispered to each other, although their voices occasionally rose loud enough to reach their comrades' ears.

A student asked, "Doesn't even one of them have a face worth seeing?"

Another answered rather sarcastically, "They're ambassadors of learning, not of passion."

A third remarked with censorious zeal as he examined the appearance of the spindly young women, "But God created them to be ambassadors of passion!"

The first youth guffawed and—motivated by a spirit of mischievous defiance—observed, "Remember we're at the university, a place where you're not allowed to mention God or passion."

"It's very logical that God wouldn't be mentioned, but passion?"

One of them responded in a reportorial tone more professional than scholarly, "This university is God's enemy, not nature's."

"What you say is true and you derive no pleasure from their sickening appearance, but this is merely the first installment of the fair sex. They'll be followed by others. The university is a new trend that will soon catch on among females. If you keep your eyes on tomorrow, it won't be long in coming."

"Do you think young women will accept the university as readily as they have the cinema, for example?"

"More readily. You'll see young women here quite unlike this sorry lot."

"And they'll press against the young men mercilessly."

"Mercy in such circumstances would be reprehensible."

"They won't try to behave, because a strong person doesn't bother to be well behaved."

"Perhaps passions will flare up between the two sexes."

"How beautiful that would be!"

"Consider the trees and the thickets: love arises there as spontaneously as maggots in jars of mish cheese."

"My Lord! Will we live to see this happy age?"

"You'll be able to wait for it if you choose."

"We're just starting and the future is dazzling."

Having finished their general comments, they began to analyze the girls individually with bitter mockery and stinging sarcasm.

* * *

Four young men walked along together slowly. They were also conversing and had probably listened with interest to the prattle of the other students. These were final year students who were almost twenty-four, and their faces shone with pride in their maturity and learning. They were not blind to their importance—or put more precisely—they were inordinately conscious of it.

Ma'mun Radwan remarked critically, "All boys talk about is girls."

Ali Taha responded to his companion's critique, "What's wrong with that? We're two halves of a whole and have been seeking each other since eternity."

Mahgub Abd al-Da'im commented, "Don't hold it against them, Mr. Ma'mun. It's Thursday, and for male students Thursday is always a day to enjoy the ladies."

Ahmad Badir, who was both a student and a journalist, smiled gently and declared oratorically, "Brothers, I invite you to state your ideas about women in a few brief words. What do you say, Mr. Ma'mun Radwan?"

The young man was perplexed. Then he smiled and asked, "Are you trying to tempt me into the type of discussion I've criticized?"

"Don't try to squirm out of it. Come on. Just a few words. I'm a journalist, and a journalist never wearies of discussion."

3

Ma'mun Radwan realized that evading Ahmad Badir would be difficult and yielded. "I say what my Lord said. If you want to know my personal take on it: woman is man's solace in this world and a level path toward solace for the next."

Ahmad Badir turned to Ali Taha and with a nod of his head asked his friend to speak. The young man said, "A woman is a man's partner in life, so they say, but—in my opinion—it should be a partnership with identical rights and obligations."

Turning toward Mahgub Abd al-Da'im, Ahmad Badir asked jocularly, "And what does our dear devil think?"

Mahgub Abd al-Da'im replied theatrically, "Woman is . . . the safety valve on the boiler."

They all laughed as they normally did when they heard one of his notions. Then they asked Ahmad Badir, "And you, what do you think?"

The young man replied dismissively, "A journalist should listen and not speak, especially nowadays."

2

They turned at the avenue's first intersection and headed toward the governorate building. Ma'mun Radwan was the tallest, although Mahgub Abd al-Da'im was almost as tall. Ali Taha was of medium height and stocky, and Ahmad Badir was quite short with a very large head. Ma'mun Radwan wanted to conclude their day's pursuits in the best possible way before greeting the day of rest. So he said in his tremulous voice, which seemed to rise straight from his heart, "Talking about women has distracted us from the topic at hand. What's your final word on the debate we just attended?"

The debate had been about principles: whether they are necessary for mankind or should be dispensed with. Addressing Ma'mun Radwan, Ali Taha said, "We both agree that man needs principles. They're the compass guiding the ship."

Mahgub Abd al-Da'im said calmly and gravely, "Tuzz."

Ali Taha, however, ignored him and continued to address Ma'mun, "Although we differ about the nature of these principles. . . ."

Shrugging his shoulders, Ahmad Badir observed, "As always!"

Ma'mun, whose eyes glittered with a fleeting light when he was excited—as at present—remarked, "All we need are the principles that God Almighty decreed."

Mahgub Abd al-Da'im commented as if astonished, "I'm stunned that a man like you believes in legends."

Ali Taha continued, "I believe in society, in the living human hive. Let's respect society's principles—on condition that we don't sanctify them—because they ought to be renewed, from one generation to the next, by scholars and educators."

Then Ahmad Badir asked him, "What principles does our generation need?"

He responded enthusiastically, "Belief in science not a spirit world, in society not paradise, in socialism not competition."

Mahgub Abd al-Da'im's critique of this statement was, "Tuzz, tuzz, tuzz."

So Ahmad Badir asked him, "And you, Mr. Mahgub: What do you have to say about the debate?"

He replied calmly, "Tuzz."

"Are principles necessary?"

"Tuzz."

"Not necessary?"

"Tuzz."

"Religion or science?"

"Tuzz."

"For which of them?"

"Tuzz."

"Don't you have some opinion?"

"Tuzz."

"Is this 'tuzz' an opinion?"

Mahgub replied with feigned calm, "It is the ultimate principle."

Ma'mun Radwan turned to Ali Taha and said, more to state

his opinion than to influence anyone, "God in the heavens and Islam on the earth. These are my principles."

Ali Taha smiled and repeated Mahgub Abd al-Da'im's previous comment, "I'm stunned that a man like you believes in legends."

Mahgub chortled, "Tuzz."

Casting a swift look at the others as they walked along, he said, "Amazing! How can a single hostel house all of us? My head is full of hot air, Mr. Ma'mun's noggin is a flask with ancient legends sealed inside it, and Ali Taha is a display of contemporary myths."

The other two ignored his comment, because they never knew when he was serious or joking and because it was tedious to debate with him, since by clowning around he evaded their attempts to pin him down.

When they could see the student hostel at the corner of Rashad Pasha Street, Ahmad Badir said goodbye and set off for the newspaper where he worked in the evening. The other three continued to the hostel to prepare for their Thursday night excursions.

3

The hostel at the corner of Rashad Pasha Street was an imposing fortress with an extensive, circular courtyard at its heart. Each of the building's three stories was a circular series of suites of rooms that opened onto a narrow corridor overlooking the court. The three friends occupied adjoining rooms on the second floor. Ma'mun Radwan went to his cramped chamber and began to change clothes. His room was furnished with a small bed and a wardrobe on the opposite wall. Between these, beneath a little window, there was a medium-sized desk with books and reference works on it. The young man loved books passionately. Thus the moment his eyes fell on Lalande's dictionary of philosophy, his lips relaxed into a delicate smile that revealed his love and enthusiasm. All the same, he lost no time. He performed his ablutions and then the afternoon prayer. Next he donned his best clothes and left his room for the street. He carried his trim body in an attractive military fashion as he set forth. He was slender without being emaciated and so light-skinned that his complexion was shot with red. His best feature was his large black eyes, which shone with a luminosity that bespoke insight, beauty, and intelligence. He marched forward, his focus distracted by nothing, his feet pounding the pavement smartly and his eyes directed toward a single goal.

Today that goal was his fiancée's home in Heliopolis. Ma'mun approached affairs of the heart with the same integrity and propriety he observed in all his dealings. He had asked for the hand of the girl, the daughter of a relative who was a high-ranking army officer, after first consulting his father. An agreement had been reached for them to marry once he finished his studies. Then he began visiting her home every Thursday. He would sit with the entire family and spend a few hours in pleasant conversation. It never occurred to him to invite his girl to the movies or to devise some stratagem for being alone with her. He simply did not believe in such modern heresies—as he put it—and deprecated them. Thus his conduct was well viewed and highly esteemed by the girl's family, which was socially conservative in their embrace of time-honored tradition.

None of this prevented his heart from beating faster when he followed his customary route. So he reached the Giza road in a few minutes and boarded the tram. When he took his customary seat—his gaze untroubled, his posture erect—his good looks and nobility were evident. Had he wished to be a lothario like Umar ibn Abi Rabi'a, he could have succeeded, but he possessed a unique blend of chastity, rectitude, and purity. He had a clean conscience and his mind was at rest. He was a pure heart who enjoyed authentic religion, deep-rooted belief, and firm morals. He had grown up in Tanta, where his father—a man of religion and moral fiber—taught in a religious institute. So he was reared in an environment that was almost Bedouin in its simplicity, religious fervor, morals, and strength. When he was young, something happened that deeply influenced his later life. He became so ill he could not attend school until he was fourteen. Thus he tasted the bitterness of solitude, experienced pain, and was refined in the furnaces of a trying ordeal. He was, however, able to study religion with his father and thus became an Islamic jurisprudent while a boy. When he entered primary school, he was an adolescent with an enormous heart, vibrant spirit, and lively intelligence. Even so, he could be bigoted and rude. In fact, he suffered from episodes of wild cruelty. During these, his soul's generosity was drained, and he would shoot up like a tongue of flame that engulfed everything it encountered and devoured anything that resisted. Then he would redouble his effort if working and plunge deeper into his devotions if praying. If he was debating something, his comments would become mean-spirited; he would be overwhelmed by despair and depression if he were alone.

In his simple life, the boy's only outlet for self-fulfillment was his work. So he outstripped all his peers and was capable of worshiping for hours on end as his tongue praised God continually. During the last days of a school year he would study twenty hours a day. He earned top marks in the third year examinations and expected to take first place on the final-year exams. To beat out everyone else became one of his top priorities—along with Islam, Arab pride, and virtue. He would allow no one else to better his performance. This competitive streak, however, left no noxious residue in his breast thanks to his extraordinary strength, great self-confidence, and firmly rooted belief in God. He brought humanism to the highest degree, and for this reason did not allow his spirituality to degenerate into sterile asceticism or self-abnegation. He used to say, "Belief means being filled with divine power in order to implement God's ideals on earth."

He was a formidable young man, even if not universally liked, since his successes made him a target for the envious and his way of life was a silent rebuke to others. Moreover, he never outgrew his preference for solitude, which had been second nature for him since his illness. Additionally, his ignorance of the principles of sociability, his dislike for humor, and a passion for candor turned his comments at times into a painful whiplash. Thus his detractors occasionally called him "the university bumpkin" or "the unexpected mahdi." A student once said of him, "Mr. Ma'mun Radwan is Islam's imam for our age. In ancient times, Amr ibn al-'As introduced Islam to Egypt, through his brilliance. Tomorrow, Ma'mun Radwan will extinguish Islam in Egypt thanks to his insensitivity." The young man remained devoted to outshining others even though he frequently feared and hated this proclivity. Yes, he feared this sense of superiority and excellence and would ask God to protect him from this evil. All the same, he failed to overcome it. Therefore he could never truly admire an important personage. So when the king opened the university he candidly announced his disdain for the government officials who attended the ceremony. For this reason too he shrugged his shoulders dismissively whenever he heard students speak enthusiastically about men they referred to as leaders. He rejected all the political parties and refused affiliation with the 'Egyptian cause.' With customary zeal, he would say, "There is only one cause: the cause of Islam in general and of the Arabs in particular."

What was truly amazing was that he was not influenced by the trend toward atheism, which was fashionable among students at the university when he was there. This can be attributed to his relatively advanced aged at the time of his enrollment at the university; he was twenty-three. By that time, he had come to believe deeply in three things he never renounced to the end of his days: God, virtue, and the cause of Islam. His vision was not distracted by the university's new light. His faith remained a boulder against which the waves of psychology, sociology, and metaphysics crashed. With his faith he defied science and philosophy in general, enlisting them as pretexts for and constituent elements of belief. How delighted he was to find preeminent philosophers under God's sway: Plato, Descartes, Pascal, and Bergson. His sincere heart welcomed the synthesis that the twentieth century promised between science, religion, and philosophy. In contemporary thought, matter dissolved into electric charges more like the spirit than earlier concepts of matter. In contemporary thought, spirituality was reclaiming its hijacked throne. In contemporary thought, scientists were preoccupied with theology and men of religion drew inspiration from science and philosophy. So blessings on the devout young philosopher! The young man in Giza did, however, differ from the sick boy in Tanta. He had grown more open-minded and magnanimous. Thus it was possible for him to listen to Mahgub Abd al-Da'im's buffoonery with a smile, to debate with Ali Taha about the relative merits of religion and atheism, and to accept the barbs of critics and scoffers—except when he became infuriated, his eyes flared, and that dread passion overwhelmed him.

Then his insight deserted him, and he might as well have been blind. The young man discovered sincere believers among his fellow students and did not feel isolated by his beliefs. Yet he never convinced anyone to share his enthusiasm for proselytizing on behalf of Islam and Arab pride. At the time, minds were full of many other concerns like the Egyptian cause, the 1923 constitution, and a boycott of foreign goods. The young man, however, never despaired at being a minority of one. It was impossible for despair to dominate a heart like his.

Great hopes excited him, but his heart was also able to embrace life and hastened to greet it with delight. Indeed, he began to gaze out of the tram window with something akin to anxiety. He wished the tram would make the trip to Heliopolis in the wink of an eye.

12

4

li Taha remained in his room until the sun began to set. He sat by the window with his eyes trained on the balcony of a small, old house that had a cigarette store at its entrance. Facing the student hostel, it stood on the corner of al-Izba Street, which was a prolongation of Rashad Pasha Street in the direction of the district of al-Doqqi. He wore his street clothes, except for his fez, and looked as trim as ever. Anyone seeing his broad shoulders would assume he was an athlete. He was a handsome young man with green eyes and blond hair that was almost golden and that suggested a distinguished pedigree. He kept anxiously watching the small, old house's balcony with expectant and apprehensive eyes until an alert vitality seized him when a girl appeared. Then he rose, waving his hands, and she smiled at him and gestured toward the street. So he donned his fez and quit first his room and then the building. He rushed to Rashad Pasha Street and then strolled along the avenue at a leisurely pace. On both sides stood lofty trees, behind which palaces and villas crouched. He began to glance back, from one moment to the next, until he saw, by the light of a peaceful sunset, the young woman from the balcony approaching with a dancing step. His heart pounding with delight, he turned and headed toward her, blushing. Then their hands met, right with left and left with right, and the young man murmured, "Welcome."

Her face resplendent with a charming smile, she murmured, "Good evening."

She gently freed her hands and took his arm. They resumed their walk toward Giza Street, keeping the pace of a loiterer out for a stroll. She was girl of eighteen, and her countenance was illuminated by ivory skin. Her black eyes' clarity and her lashes had a special magic. Her jet-black hair combined with her fair complexion to dazzle the eye. Her gray overcoat enclosed a supple, ripe body diffusing enchantment and radiance. They walked along slowly, their youth and vitality providing a delightful sight. Ali Taha began to scout the street cautiously as if expecting to be taken unaware, while the girl, who waited with joyful desire, observed him circumspectly until the youth was reassured that no one was watching. Then placing his fingers beneath her chin he drew her face toward him and planted his lips on hers in a juicy kiss. Afterward he raised his head with a profound sigh and they silently continued their walk. She noticed that he was examining her carefully and remembered, despite the magic and enchantment of the scene, that her coat was almost worn out. Then her delight faded. Without meaning to, she asked, "Do you dislike seeing this old coat all the time?"

The young man's disapproval was apparent in his expression. He chided her, "How can you heed such trifles? The coat encompasses a treasure that has made it a lucky omen for me."

She did not agree with him that the coat was a "trifle." Indeed, she had repeatedly told herself regretfully: a happy life means being young and well dressed. Noticing his elegant wool suit, she felt like scolding him. So she said, "What a rascal you are! Do you think clothes are unimportant when you're so proud of your elegance?"

He blushed, looking like a bewildered child. Then he said apologetically, "The suit's new. You can't buy an old suit, but clothes are insignificant incidentals. Isn't that so, darling?"

All the same, she feared starting a discussion with him, because he would leap at the chance for a debate and saw himself as her instructor, an assumption that made her uncomfortable. In point of fact, he did harbor contradictory positions. He frequently disparaged the importance of clothing, fine foods, and the class system but remained particular about how he dressed, ate gourmet food till he was satiated, and spent freely. Ihsan Shihata, however, had something to say, something she knew he was waiting to hear. So in her melodious, flirtatious voice she remarked, "I've almost finished the book you lent me."

His interest was apparent from his expression; he wanted to love her mind as much as he loved her person. He asked, "What do you think?"

She replied candidly, "I only understood a little of it and couldn't do much with that."

Disappointed, he asked, "Why?"

Smiling at him to lighten the impact of her words, she explained, "The gist of this book, which you call a story, is ideas and opinions. What I look for in books is life and emotion."

"But life is thought and emotion!"

She summoned all her courage to say, "Don't try to tie me down with your logic, for I may not be able to defend myself against it, but that won't change my taste. In my opinion, music is the true measure of art. Any part of a book that goes beyond the range of music should not be considered art at all."

Her opinion appalled him. He smiled wanly and said regretfully, "You're depriving yourself of the tastiest fruit of true art."

She laughingly replied, "*Magdeleine, The Sorrows of Young Werther*, the suffering figures of Raphael—these are the masterpieces I like."

She made this remark in the tone of someone quoting the Qur'an to the effect, "*You have your religion and I have mine.*" So the young man fell silent, wondering whether he would really have to renounce changing her opinion. He sincerely wished for them to love each other with their hearts and their minds, for their lives to mesh perfectly, and for him to find in her a lover, colleague, and respected peer. His love for her dominated his heart and soul, but he aspired to fashion her over time into a spouse of a type unknown till then in Eastern households. Their stroll took them as far as Giza Street, where they turned left. The young man sighed with relief, because the street was almost deserted and the weather was fairly overcast. He raised her hand to his mouth and kissed it passionately. Then turning toward her he calmly helped himself to a sweet kiss from her full, tender lips. When he noticed that she closed her eyelids in response to the kiss, his powerful body trembled and sparks of delight shot through his spirit. Swallowing, he said, "How sweet you are . . . how beautiful!"

A delicious moment of delectable magic flitted past. Then he sighed and said somewhat regretfully, "I only have a few short months before the final exam. How about you?"

She replied, "The baccalaureate is in June. Where do you think I should study?"

The youth said enthusiastically, "My faculty."

Although straitened circumstances forced her to complete her education, she would have liked him to say, for example, "You've studied enough. Let's make a nest for ourselves." She asked him with a certain reserve, "Why should I choose your department?"

"So we can become a single mind with an identical craft and career."

"The same career?"

He said with undiminished enthusiasm, "Yes, darling. A woman's job is far more important than being a homemaker. It's impossible for me to betray my principles or for me to consent to deprive society of a beautiful and useful contributor like you."

She knew he was right on the one hand, because financial need dictated that she should choose a career some day, although his enthusiasm for his own opinion—for some reason—annoyed her. She would have preferred to be the one who forced him to accept this idea over his hesitation and objections.

They continued along the deserted street, drawing inspiration for their conversation, which was punctuated by kisses, from their dreams.

Ihsan Shihata was supremely conscious of two things: her beauty and her poverty. Her beauty was astounding. The hostel's residents had fallen prey to it, and the rooms' inhabitants had begun to broadcast the fervor of their souls, which all focused on the small, dilapidated house's balcony, where they abandoned themselves at the feet of the beautiful, vainglorious girl. Her home lacked a mirror that could truly reflect this graceful beauty, however, because poverty was an equally conspicuous reality. Her seven young brothers strengthened her consciousness of it, especially since they all depended on the income from the cigarette store, which was only one meter square, with a clientele composed predominantly of students. She had long feared the consequences of poverty's outrages, including poor nutrition, on her beauty. As a matter of fact, had it not been for the recipes of her mother, who before she married Master Shihata Turki had been one of the singers based on Muhammad Ali Street, she would have grown skinny and her rump, which a poet from the College of Medicine had celebrated in a resounding ode, would have withered. When she met Ali Taha, her heart had chosen him out of all the residents of the student hostel. His youth, good looks, noble pedigree, and promising future excited her admiration. Two important matters, however, contended for control of her heart from the word go: her romantic life and her family life. Put another way, the struggle was between Ali Taha and her seven young brothers. Before Ali Taha, a wealthy young law student had courted her. Sensing from his conduct that he sought amusement for his heart and entertainment for his youth, she had remained on guard with him. Her parents were fully informed about all the secrets of her life, and the only thing that alarmed her was her mother's prodding and her father's greedy concern with the young man's fortune. Thus she came face-to-face with the bitter realities of her life and its grievous truths. As a matter of fact, her parents had no moral scruples. Before evolving into marriage, their relationship had been a passionate affair. Her father had made a living from his good looks and impudence until her mother married him and gave him her life savings to invest. Then he squandered most of this on drugs and gambling till he was left with only the cigarette shop. Even so he would console himself by reflecting, "It's true that my life's been a waste, but Ihsan's a blessing." The girl discovered that he and her mother were Satan's willing allies plotting her downfall. She was in no hurry to fall, however. She took offense at any unintentional slight, and her alert pride saved her. She saw her young boyfriend sitting with her father one day in the shop and realized that they were haggling over her virtue. Feeling disgraced and dishonored, she became furious and broke off with the youth so brutally that he was left without hope. She emerged victorious from this experience, but only after learning that she lived in an abyss. She was also conscious deep inside of being liberated suddenly from all supervision or restraint. She was now free to do whatever she wanted without any explanation. Her consciousness of this total freedom created a revolution within her soul, and she remained for a time without any goal—or obstacle for that matter. A wild awakening, however, spread through her emotions and surfaced, even though modesty and caution restrained them. If the atmosphere was stifling, her lungs were healthy. Her circumstances suggested an inevitable conclusion, a done deal. Her dissolute father commented to her sorrowfully on the loss of the wealthy young man, "You're responsible for all of us, especially your seven brothers." Good Lord, how would she be able to shape her own future when faced by such corrupt impulses? Couldn't her parents counsel each other to be patient till she finished her studies at the teacher training institute and found an honorable job to support herself? She had surrendered to the fates without confidence or belief, the way weak-willed people do, until Ali Taha came along. With Ali she found true affection, powerful sincerity, and a lofty goal. So he provided support for her tottering willpower and rescued her from a flood of anxiety and fear, restoring to her a feeling of self-respect and pride. She fell in love with him and hung her hopes on him. Master Shihata Turki regarded the new young man with displeasure, saying of him, "He's a poor fellow; he doesn't even smoke!" He once told the girl sarcastically, "Congratulations on the handsome young man whom God has sent to starve us to death!" She ignored her father, however, and placed her hopes on the future, which bore responsibility for providing a respectable career for her and realizing her heart's dreams.

Now Ali Taha was a young man with many fine points. He was a good example of someone with true social consciousness. In secondary school he had been a distinguished member of the advanced placement division, the school outings association, the debate team, and the student newspaper. He had excelled in debate, oratory, cooking, and singing and had exhibited a commendable enthusiasm for inquiry and culture and a sincere allegiance to virtue. On entering the university, the field of his activities narrowed but deepened and matured. He became Mr. Ali, the president of the Debate Society, and was distinguished from his peers by his oratorical prowess, his broad cultural grounding, and his quick wit. He was interested in ideals and spoke with zeal and conviction about the virtuous city. Those who knew him believed him, but some critics spread a rumor that he was a rascal worse than any other, that cloaked in virtue he raided every circle merely to chase beautiful women in the name of science and virtue, and that he discussed ethics the way a matchmaker discusses a bride she has never seen. But they exaggerated and lied. The truth was that the young man was sincere and truthful and that if he loved beauty, he loved it respectfully and sincerely. All the same, his life had seen its share of violent crises, because his religious faith had been shaken and exposed to deadly pains of transformation since the beginning of his university life. Still he was courageous and truthful. So he welcomed his new life with an enthusiastic will and an intellect obsessed with the truth. He was not a sneering buffoon and did not hide his admiration for Ma'mun Radwan's truthfulness and courage. He, however, threw himself into the embrace of materialist philosophy. So although he read Hegel, he also read natural scientists like Ostwald and Mach. He adopted a materialist explanation of life and felt totally comfortable with the claims that existence is matter, that life and spirit are complex material processes, and that consciousness is a characteristic but inconsequential attribute comparable to the sound a wheel makes while revolving without itself having any effect of its own. Ma'mun Radwan kept telling him that materialist philosophy was an easy philosophy but one that failed to solve even a single problem in a satisfactory way. Ali Taha, however, was a socially active young man who did not have the patience for lengthy reflection. He would take a week to study what Ma'mun covered in two days. The time he spent reading had to be balanced against periods for sports, debate, travel, love, and so forth. This comprehensive materialist explanation was enough philosophy to allow him to get on with his life. There was, however, one practical difficulty that threatened to become a major stumbling block: ethics. In the past his ethical system had been buttressed by religion. So what could support it today? If not God, what could sustain the value of the virtues? Or, should he scorn them the way he scorned his former belief system and throw himself into life's torrential current without any anchor or conscience? The logic was straightforward and the conclusion preordained, but he hesitated, held himself back, and was leery about letting himself go. He asked himself whether it would not be possible to live the way Abu al-Ala' al-Ma'arri had. Abu al-Ala', however, had been blind, pockmarked, and melancholy, whereas he was a handsome young man with rippling muscles and a social temperament. So how could he embrace asceticism and the simple life? He found himself in the same confusion that Ihsan Shihata did following her liberation from her parents' supervision. Finally Ali Taha discovered in Auguste Comte his savior, just as Ihsan Shihata found hers in Ali Taha. This philosopher brought him the glad tidings of a new god (society) and of a new religion (science). He believed in human society and human science and held the conviction that the atheist—like the monotheist—has principles and ideals if he so chooses and his volition follows suit, and that good has more profound roots in human nature than in religion. Mankind had created religion in ancient times; religion had not produced mankind as he had once imagined. He began to say of himself, "I used to be virtuous because of religion,

21

but mindlessly so. Today I'm virtuous because of my mind and without the superstition." He returned to his ideals self-confidently and devotedly, filled with zeal, force, and a passion for social reform, dreaming of a terrestrial paradise. So he studied social theorists till he felt comfortable calling himself a socialist. Thus his spiritual peregrinations, which had begun in Mecca, terminated in Moscow. At one point he yearned to attract his closest friends to socialism, but the attempt failed. Ahmad Badir told him apologetically, "I'm a Wafdist journalist, and the Wafd is a capitalist party." Ma'mun Radwan told him with typical conviction, "Islam has a sensible type of socialism. It has zakat, which guarantees social justice, if scrupulously observed, without suppressing the instincts from which man draws support for his struggle. If you desire a world system that prepares for true brotherhood and happiness, Islam awaits you." Mahgub Abd al-Da'im merely shrugged his shoulders and replied tersely, "Tuzz." All the same, Ali Taha had discovered a goal that preserved him from anxiety, anarchy, and depravity. He had a right to say of himself happily, "Here's my identity card, which needs no explanation: poor and socialist, atheist and honorable, a Platonic lover."

5

Mahgub Abd al-Da'im also waited in his room but did not change his clothes, because unlike his two friends he did not own a special outfit for Thursday night. Since he was watching the street from his window, he saw Ma'mun Radwan leave the hostel with his military gait, noticed the love signal from the balcony of the small, old house, and then saw the two young lovers accompany each other to Rashad Pasha Street. He bade each of them farewell with a 'tuzz' replete with sarcasm and resentment, because his sarcasm always harbored some resentment. He too was waiting for a rendezvous but preferred the dark and loved dissimulation. So the hostel was virtually empty except for him. Like Ma'mun Radwan, Mahgub Abd al-Da'im was tall and lean, but he had a sallow complexion and frizzy hair. His face was distinguished by protruding, honey-colored eyes and jutting eyebrows. Along with all this, the gleam of his anxious, mercurial glance suggested defiant irony. Unlike his two friends, he was not good looking, although there was nothing repulsively ugly about his features either. A

23

person observing him would not miss the most challenging aspect of his appearance: his mouth that remained slightly open, as if he might hurl a wisecrack, taunt, or mordant remark at his interlocutor. Thinking his life was filled with problems, he placed at the head of the list his sexual difficulties, which he described succinctly as a problem as hard to resolve as the Egyptian 'question.' He saw Ihsan Shihata, who had long excited the volcano of his desire—just as he saw every other woman—as breast, butt, and legs. Even one of these charming features was enough to release an electric charge in his chest. The girl, however, according to his stated opinion, had made a wise choice in preferring the blond youth with green eyes. His own life continued to be forlorn and lonely. So his heart was gloomy and his mind in continual revolt. He had borrowed his philosophy of life from various thinkers, according to his whims. His philosophy was freedom as he understood the concept, and 'tuzz' was its most accurate watchword. His philosophy called for liberation from everything: from values, ideals, belief systems and principles, from social culture as a whole. He would tell himself sarcastically, "Since my family won't leave me anything that gladdens me, I shouldn't inherit anything from them that saddens me." He would also say, "The truest equation in the world is: religion + science + philosophy + ethics = tuzz." He explained systems of philosophy with a cynical logic that matched his desires. He would marvel at Descartes' statement, "I think, therefore I am" and agree with him that the soul is the basis of existence. Next he would say that his soul was the most important thing in existence and that its happiness was all that mattered. He also liked the social theorists' claim that societies create all their ethical and religious values. Thus he thought it ignorant and stupid to allow a principle or value to block his soul's pursuit of happiness. Even if science had prepared the way for his liberation from figments of the imagination, this did not mean he believed in it or that he should devote his life to it. His plan was rather to exploit science and benefit from it. He was as sarcastic about scientists as about theologians. His objective in life was pleasure and power, achieved by the easiest routes and means, without any regard for morality, religion, or virtue. His acceptance of this philosophy had been guided by his passions, but he had worked his way to this point over the years. His childhood was shaped by the street and by his native gifts, because his parents were good but uneducated people. Their circumstances dictated that he spent his formative years on the streets of the city of al-Qanatir. His playmates were shrewd lads who obeyed their natural instincts, unrestrained by oversight or manners. So he cursed, called people names, assaulted and was assaulted, and went from bad to worse. When he moved to a new setting—school—he began to realize that he was living a foul life, and his soul suffered bitter disgrace, fear, anxiety, and rebellion. Then he found himself in a new environment once again as a student at the university. He observed around him cultured young men who nourished lofty hopes and high ideals. He likewise stumbled upon eccentric trends and ideas that had never before crossed his mind. He came across fashionable atheism and theories popularized by psychologists, sociologists, and scholars of human conduct and other social phenomena. He derived a demonic pleasure from all this, assembling from the dregs a personal philosophy that satisfied his heart, which had previously been enervated by a feeling of inferiority. Formerly an inconsequential fallen rogue, in the twinkling of an eye he became a philosopher. Society was an ancient sorcerer that had declared some things virtues and others vices. Now that he had learned society's secret and mastered its sorcery, would he turn virtues into vices and vices into virtues? He rubbed his hands together with delight, recalling his past positively and gazing into his future with a

25

sense of promise, and freed himself from his feelings of inferiority. From the outset, however, he realized that he would need to keep his philosophy secret. It was possible for Ma'mun Radwan to advocate Islam publicly. It was appropriate for Ali Taha to announce his adoption of free thought and socialism. Mahgub's philosophy, though, had to remain secret, not out of respect for public opinion (contempt for everything was one of its principles) but because it would only bear fruit if he were the sole convert. If everyone aspired to be vicious, he would obviously lose his edge of superiority. For this reason, he kept it to himself and did not even proclaim fashionable aspects of it like atheism and free thought. If he felt stressed or desolate he would relieve his heart with sarcastic mockery. So people thought him a clown rather than a criminally predisposed demon. He went about his business, poverty-stricken and amoral, scouting for opportunities and pouncing on them with boundless audacity.

※

He stayed in his room, waiting for it to get dark. His heart had had its share of adventures, but his love, like his philosophy, could not survive the light of day. His girlfriend was by profession a cigarette butt collector. He was infuriated by his luck in love, but what could he do when his funds barely sufficed for life's necessities? He would frequently mock himself, saying, "I'm no better than she is. She recycles leftover tobacco and I recycle leftover philosophy. Furthermore, society thinks worse of me than of her." He consoled himself, "When a man humbles himself before God, God raises him." Chance had cast her his way, and he had not allowed this opportunity to escape. One evening when he was walking along al-Izba Street, which was deserted, he spotted her behind a fig tree with a doorman from Rashad Pasha Street. He lay in wait for her until he saw her leave by herself after the

Nubian doorman had returned to the other street. Then he accosted her with his normal audacity and, touching her shoulder, said with a smile, "I saw everything."

The girl stopped and stared at him with amazement. He examined her by the streetlight and discovered that she was dark brown and had swelling breasts. He started panting and eyed her like a predatory leopard. The girl snapped out of her astonished daze and asked him disdainfully, "What did you see?"

Mahgub's eyes told her, "Everything!" but he replied, "A fig tree, the doorman."

With the same disdainful tone she asked, "What do you want?"

He said in a tormented voice, "The same."

"Where?"

"How about the same place?"

She turned back but declared in an admonitory tone before proceeding any further, "Three piasters!"

He murmured with relief, "Fine."

The price was a pittance and would not upset his budget. Moreover the girl had swelling breasts. He merely hoped that the dark brown was her natural color and not layers of dirt and that all he needed to worry about was her body's foul odor. Never mind; something was better than nothing, and could he forget that he himself had—back in al-Qanatir—bathed only for festivals? Indeed, he asked himself, "Don't all women look alike in the dark?" When they were finished, he asked, "Have you been going with that doorman a long time?"

"No. This was the first night."

"Didn't you arrange another meeting?"

"Certainly not."

Mahgub said with relief, "But this won't be our last night."

While arranging the veil around her head, she murmured, "Gladly."

※

Although darkness was swallowing the world, he remained at his station by the window, waiting for his rendezvous with his girl-friend. Then he heard a knock at the door and sauntered to open it. He saw the hostel's concierge waving a letter at him. He took it and shut the door again. Casting a quick glance at the envelope he saw that it had been posted in al-Qanatir. Then he noticed easily that the handwriting was not his father's. Who could be writing him? He had not seen this handwriting before.

6

He opened the envelope in astonishment and read the following.

Young Master Mahgub Effendi Abd al-Da'im:
May you enjoy God's peace and compassion.
We are sad to inform you that your dear father is ill and bedridden. We ask God to provide a satisfactory outcome, but you must come as quickly as possible to reassure yourself about his condition. They asked me to write you this letter. So don't delay. Peace.

Shalabi al-Afash
(Proprietor of the Grocery Store of
al-Qanatir al-Khayriya)

This meant that his father was too ill to hold a pen. What had happened to him? As he read the letter a second time, apprehension showed on his pallid face and caused him to tug on his left eyebrow. The amazing thing was that he never remembered his father complaining of ill health a single day. His body had always been strong and his step firm. No doubt a grave illness had gotten the better of him and debilitated him. Mahgub wondered what the future concealed for him. What did it have in store for him and his mother?

But it was wrong to waste time with pointless conjectures or to delay his journey even a minute. He scribbled a note to Ma'mun Radwan explaining his sudden departure, wrapped his gallabiya in an old newspaper, and then left the hostel. He did not head to al-Izba Street as he had been longing to do minutes before. Instead he took Rashad Pasha Street, or Ali-and-Ihsan's street, as he called it sarcastically. He proceeded to tell himself: If the man's time has come, all my hopes will be buried alive. My Lord! Is it possible that this is happening when I'm only four months from the final examination? He hurried down that deserted street where the mansions were sunk in majestic silence, hearing only the sound of his footsteps till he reached Giza Street and boarded the tram. Melancholy cast a shadow over his face and eyes. Sitting there grief-stricken, his mind turned to the two friends closest to him: Ma'mun Radwan and Ali Taha. He envied them their contentment and confidence. Ma'mun Radwan's father taught in the institutes and had a nice salary—so his family did not live in the shadow of fear. He gave his son more than enough. If it were not for Ma'mun's stupidity, which caused him to devote his life to learning and worship, he would have enjoyed life's pleasures. But he was stupid, and stupid people are always lucky. Ali Taha's father was a translator for the city of Alexandria and received a huge salary. His friend was not immune to life's pleasures, within the limits set by his ideals. He was a happy young man. All he needed to be happy was Ihsan. Possibly no other person so excited Mahgub's envy as this handsome, successful young man. Whereas he . . . he was wretched! His father—do you suppose he still had a father?—was a clerk in a Greek-owned creamery in al-Qanatir. He had worked there for twenty-five years and earned eight pounds. If he stopped working, he would only be recompensed for a few more months. The man allocated three pounds to him every month during the academic year. This sum covered necessities like housing, food, and clothing, and the young man was grudgingly satisfied, though he eyed Cairo's pleasures from afar, eavesdropping on news of them with woeful avidity. His unruly passion blended with unbridled ambition. These ideas occurred to him in succession, spoiling that hour more than ever before. Then, oblivious to the vistas of fields and waterways that the tram afforded in its speedy transit, he thought about his relationship with the two young men and what people call friendship. Did he really have a friend? Certainly not; what was friendship if not one of the virtues he scorned? He actually was partial to them. Ma'mun's debates attracted him, and Ali's spirit endeared him to Mahgub. He enjoyed spending time with them, discussing and debating, but what did all that have to do with friendship? Besides, he envied and despised them. He would not hesitate to destroy them if he found that to his advantage. He proceeded to say, as if egging himself on, "Total freedom, total tuzz. Let me take Satan for my role model—the perfect symbol for total perfection. He represents true rebellion, true arrogance, true ambition, and a revolt against all principles." The tram's last stop was al-Is'af, where he got off and boarded another tram for Maydan al-Mahatta. Then he entered the train station itself and rushed to the third-class window to buy a ticket. When he moved away from the window he found himself face-to-face with a young man who was in his thirties, of medium build, on the short side, and somewhat portly, with a large, triangular face, thick eyebrows, penetrating gaze, and round eyes, and who was casting a completely self-confident, vain and supercilious look at everything around him. Recognizing this fellow, Mahgub approached, holding out his hand and calling out respectfully, "Mr. Salim al-Ikhshidi! Greetings."

He turned toward Mahgub without altering his expression, which he rarely modified, for he was not surprised or startled and looked neither glad nor sad. Whenever he wished to express his anger, which he frequently did, he would speak in a rude tone of voice. Turning toward Mahgub, he said with calm composure, "How are you, Mahgub?"

"Thanks to you and praise to God! But, sir, what brings you to the railway station?"

Al-Ikhshidi replied in his composed voice, "I'm traveling to our hometown, al-Qanatir, to visit my father. But what brings you? It's not time for your vacation."

Mahgub said with obvious sorrow, "I'm heading to al-Qanatir as well to tend to my sick father."

"Abd al-Da'im Effendi's ill? May God restore his health! Give him my greetings."

Then they walked side by side to the platform for al-Qanatir. Not having heard any news of al-Ikhshidi for some time, Mahgub asked, "Sir, are you still Qasim Bey Fahmi's secretary?"

Al-Ikhshidi, whose eyes showed the hint of a smile, replied, "I've now been nominated to become his office manager. The memo is with personnel."

Mahgub responded with unalloyed delight, "Congratulations, congratulations, sir!"

Raising his eyebrows arrogantly, the other man added tersely, "Level five."

Mahgub exclaimed, "Congratulations, congratulations! Next it will be level four!"

Al-Ikhshidi said philosophically, "Our country has been plundered and looted. Its affairs are in the hands of weak fools. No matter how high we advance, it will always be less than we deserve."

Mahgub endorsed this statement, remarking, "That's true, sir."

Then al-Ikhshidi excused himself and headed toward the first-class carriage. The young man watched till he disappeared. So he made his way to third class, his distress and his dreams both visible in his expression. He took a seat in the coach, his mind reflecting busily, al-Ikhshidi never far from his thoughts. Two years before, al-Ikhshidi had been a final-year student just as he, Mahgub, was now. Perhaps he too had lost his belief in principles, only without broadcasting that fact or making a fuss about it. Perhaps there was no fundamental difference between the two of them. Intellectually and morally—or amorally—they were the same. Their temperaments, however, were quite different. Salim al-Ikhshidi weighed his words carefully, and Mahgub had never heard him disparage any principle or ethical maxim. Mahgub, on the other hand, despite his caution, made fun of everything. Something that Mahgub remembered and would not forget was that his acquaintance was known toward the end of his university years as an important student leader, a hero of the boycott committees, and a distributor of pamphlets opposing the new constitution. He also remembered that al-Ikhshidi was once invited to meet the minister. Many predictions were made about the meeting, and many people expected that some injustice or outrage would occur. Instead, the young man did an abrupt about-face and withdrew entirely from politics, terminating his previously boundless activities. From that time on he was seen only in lecture halls. If anyone asked him the secret behind this transformation, he would reply as coolly as ever, "The real arena for student activism is learning!" When he received his degree, he was appointed to government service—ahead of the top students—to serve as Qasim Bey Fahmi's secretary, sponsored by the minister himself. Moreover, he started at the sixth level, which at that time seemed a mythical paradise. Now he was a candidate for the fifth level, less than two years after his first appointment—long after the minister who had recruited him had resigned. This fact showed that he had earned the trust of Qasim Bey himself and would continue to advance. What a role model! He certainly was a man who deserved admiration and envy. The glory of his post and his prosperity clearly set him apart. So what if Ma'mun Radwan and Ali Taha despised him? Tuzz.

The train barreled along, and cold air penetrated the interior, even though the windows were shut tight. He only became conscious of the chill, however, when he reached the end of this series of reflections. So he buttoned his jacket and sat up straight. He quickly recalled his father's illness and realized that he had been exploring dreams while ignoring the abyss before him. His gloom returned. He looked about sorrowfully and dejectedly till the train stopped at al-Qanatir. Then he collected his parcel and disembarked. As he quit the station for the street, he cast a comprehensive look at the town and cried out, "Qanatir, our city, may you distribute good fortune equitably among all your citizens!"

7

*I*n just a few minutes he found himself in front of the small house where he had been born—a one-story structure with a yard enclosed by wooden stakes in front. The look of the place suggested not merely simplicity but squalor.

The house was on the opposite side of the street from the train station. Its flat roof offered a view of the fields beyond the tracks. The house was plunged into darkness, except for a gleam of light emanating from a gap at his father's window. His heart would not stop pounding, and fear and hope clashed inside him. He crossed the front yard to the door and knocked gently. Then he heard the clop of wooden clogs. Recognizing the step, he opened the door, where the apparition stood. He drew nearer, saying, "Good evening, Mother."

He heard a voice sigh, "You!" Then she took his hand between hers and asked in the same exhausted voice, "How are you, son? My heart told me it was you."

The hall was so dark that he could not make out her features. Closing the door, he asked anxiously, "Mother, what happened? How's my father?"

The woman replied in a mournful voice, "May our Lord take him by the hand."

He placed the parcel containing his gallabiya on a table and entered his father's room with wary steps. His eyes examined the man, who was stretched out on the bed. Then he approached him. The man's head was tilted toward the wall. Mahgub mumbled faintly, "Good evening, Father. How are you?"

His father gave no indication that he had heard or understood anything. So his mother leaned over and said, "Mahgub's greeting you."

The man slowly moved his head round and opened his eyelids. Then he extended his left hand, which Mahgub took between both of his and kissed. The man looked very ill, and his eyes were clouded, as though oozing a foul liquid. His mouth was contorted too.

Mahgub asked, "Father, how are you? All power flows from God."

The man rested his eyes on him and, speaking in a voice that came in spurts and sounded almost like a death rattle, replied, "Noon today was the first time I spoke again."

Mahgub felt alarmed and asked his mother, "Was he unable to speak for a time?"

The exhausted woman said, "Yes, son. He was at work last Tuesday afternoon as usual. He suddenly fell down and lost the ability to speak. They carried him here and called the doctor. He came, cupped him, and gave him an injection. He continues to visit him every morning. His ability to speak returned only before noon today."

"What did the doctor say?"

The look in her eyes was anxious, and her lips moved without making any sound. Then his father said, "He said it is paralysis . . . partial . . . paralysis."

The young man was alarmed by this hideous word, even though he was totally ignorant of its medical implications. Wishing to allay his fears, his mother observed, "But he stressed this morning that the danger has passed."

In his staccato, slurred speech, the father continued, "I . . . understand . . . what was said. . . . I'll never be the same."

Biting his lip, Mahgub asked his mother, "Did this happen without any warning?"

"No, son. Your father was in the best of health—as we've always known him—but then his right leg began to feel heavy and he had a headache Monday night."

Everyone was silent. Then the invalid closed his eyes and stopped moving, as if he had fallen into a sound slumber. The young man turned his head toward his mother and realized at once that she had not slept a wink since Tuesday evening. Her eyes were red, lackluster, and encircled by blue halos, and her skin was pale. He was overcome by sorrow and grief. His parents seemed creatures as miserable as he was. He sat down on a chair near the bed, bowed his head, and reflected: This family's destiny depends on the life of a ruined man. What's beneath those sealed eyelids: life or death? Success or homelessness? Why didn't this stroke wait a year? He recalled silent, majestic Rashad Pasha Street: the mansions on either side of it, the pashas and beys transported back and forth to it in automobiles, and the women who could be glimpsed from behind curtains or between the shrubbery. How did his wretched parents compare to all those people? And this dilapidated house! He began to tell himself that if he were the heir to one of those mansions and his father—the pasha—was on the brink of death, he would be waiting impatiently for his demise. He sighed from a wounded heart where rage flared. Then he asked himself, his head still bowed: I wonder how this tragedy will end?

❈

He looked stealthily at his mother, who was seated by his feet with her head bowed. He saw that she was enveloped by the black clothing she had sworn she would always wear in memory of his two sisters, who had died of typhoid. Her face was withered, and she looked older than her age, which was a little over fifty. She had succumbed to the burdens of a life spent by the flame of the cookstove and heat of the oven—kneading dough, baking, washing, and sweeping. Her fingers were worn to the bone and the veins stood out on the back of her hands. She had lacked any opportunity for small talk during her life. She resembled the invisible fuel powering a large engine. She loved her son to the point of adoration, and this affection had doubled after his two siblings died in the bloom of childhood. Even so, she had not exerted any noticeable influence on his development. She had never had anyone she could talk to and had lived in silent ignorance as if mute. His father's circumstances similarly had obliged him to withdraw from his son's life. He worked nonstop at the firm from morning till after supper. Then he hurried off to Sufi dhikr circles, where he chanted till midnight. Thus he barely saw his son. He was a serious, indefatigable man, loyal to his chums and a good representative and reflection of them. He took pride in his kinship to a major bureaucrat—a relative of his wife's. Like her, he never enjoyed any free time. He was not sustained by his marriage, and his supervision of his son was limited to forcing him to observe some of his religion's duties—with frequent recourse to the stick. For all these reasons, Mahgub had feared his father while growing up and fled to the street where his upbringing and formation were completed. Thus his tie to his parents was weak and frayed. He loved his mother more than his father but remained ready to sacrifice his relationship to his parents in keeping with his nihilistic philosophy, which had no basis whatsoever. He did not grieve for his father as much as he felt anxious about the man who allocated three pounds to him each month.

8

On the morning of the second day, the physician came, examined the patient, and gave him an injection of camphor. Then he declared his satisfaction with the condition of his patient, who was definitely out of danger. Mahgub followed the man out of the room and caught up with him in the yard. The doctor turned toward him, realizing why he had trailed after him. "I told your father the truth. The stroke was partial; otherwise it would have been fatal. All the same, I told him just as candidly that he won't be able to return to work. He'll remain in bed for a few months. He should regain control of his paralyzed side. Indeed, he may even walk again."

Mahgub stopped paying attention when he heard, "He won't be able to return to work." He grasped none of what was said after that. The world went dark. He returned to his father's room, stunned. His father had a practical nature and never let a matter hang in suspense if he could say something to resolve it. So he told his son to come to his bedside and said in his slurred speech, "Listen, son. I won't return to my position at the firm. That's a fact. What do you think?"

Mahgub felt even more dejected. He remained silent waiting for the verdict, so the man continued, "Perhaps the company will pay me a small settlement. That will inevitably run out after a few months. Indeed, the safest assumption is that nothing will remain of it after three or four months at most. But I still have contacts who can find you work that can support all of us."

Mahgub replied entreatingly, his eyes filled with pain and despair, "Father, the exam's coming up soon. This is January, and it's in May. If I take a job now, it won't be as a university graduate. That would mean a big loss for my future."

His father replied sorrowfully, "I know, but what alternative is there? I'm afraid we'll be humiliated or starve."

The young man begged fervently in a forceful, zealous voice, "Four months, just four months between me and the fruit of fifteen years of work. Give me a chance, Father. The settlement will last us till I can stand on my own two feet. We won't go hungry. We won't be humiliated, God willing."

"What will become of us if your calculations are wrong? What if your effort is in vain—God forbid. Our lives are in your hands."

Clinging desperately to hope, Mahgub responded, "You don't know, Father, how hard I'll work! Nothing's going to come between me and success!"

The young man hesitated a moment before commenting, "And then there's my mother's relative Ahmad Bey Hamdis!"

His father raised his left hand to object and frowned disapprovingly. The young man feared that he had annoyed his father and that all his persuasion would fail. So he quickly said, "We don't need anyone's assistance. Matters will turn out as I hope, God willing." He realized it had been a mistake to mention the name of their august relative, who had slighted them and scorned his tie to them ever since ascending to his lofty post. Yes, Mahgub's father publicly boasted to strangers of the relationship but frequently criticized the man in Mahgub's mother's presence and normally disdained and condemned him. Mahgub regretfully realized this and added, "We don't need anyone's assistance. We just need to be patient and to seek reassurance from God's mercy. Just four months and then relief!"

His father knew that his settlement would last them—with penny-pinching—five or six months. He reflected for a time and then asked, "Could you live on *one pound* a month?"

One pound. That's what his room at the hostel cost. Good Lord! Yesterday the world seemed difficult when he had three pounds to spend. How would he manage tomorrow with only one pound? His father was merciless and added, "We have no alternative. The decision's in your hands."

Did he really have a choice? Definitely not. His father was in a tight spot. All Mahgub could do was to yield and submit.

"As you wish."

The old man said, "As God wishes. God, who is responsible for granting you success in whatever is for the best, will deliver us from our helpless condition."

The man suggested that his son should return to Cairo that evening to avoid losing any more time when he was most in need of it. So the young man said goodbye to his parents, kissed his father's hand, and allowed his mother to kiss and bless him. As he started to leave the room, he heard his father say, "God be with you. Work hard and trust in God. Don't forget: you are our only hope."

He headed for the train station. No matter how things stood, he had been delivered from the anxiety that had consumed him on his arrival. He now knew that his hopes hung from a thread that had yet to be severed. He would figure out how to handle the ordeals the future had in store for him, no matter what the cost. He listlessly bade his hometown goodbye and took his seat in the train. He quickly forgot his house and family, thinking only of himself. As he plucked a hair from his left eyebrow, he asked why he had been born in that household. What had he inherited from his parents besides ignominy, poverty, and homeliness? Why had he been bound by those shackles before he even saw the light of day? Had he been the son of Hamdis Bey, for example, he would have had a different physique, face, and fortune. He surely would have known contentment and peace of mind. He would have acquired a car. He brooded sorrowfully about the poverty that lay in wait for him. He saw its mocking smile, which seemed to tell him, "You couldn't fend me off when you had three pounds. How can you repel me with only one?" Where would he live? How would he eat? He shook his head in consternation without feeling any lessening or diminution of his worries. He was supremely self-assured and daring to the nth degree, although irascible and splenetic.

9

He caught sight of Rashad Pasha Street when the sun was dissolving into a bloody lake of twilight and darkness was already shading the edges of the horizons. Chancing to look round as he turned onto the street, he saw Ali Taha coming from the university. So he stopped to wait for him. They shook hands and then Ali said with concern, "Mr. Ma'mun told me your father was ill. I felt really sad. Your prompt return tempts me to think you're reassured and that makes me happy."

Mahgub did not want anyone to learn about his woes. So, smiling, he replied tersely, "Thanks."

"He is better, isn't he?"

"Certainly, thanks."

They walked along slowly, side-by-side, as though out for a stroll. Mahgub wondered whether his companion was returning from or heading toward a romantic tryst. Ali afforded him as many reasons to feel delight as pain. He glanced stealthily at him and found he was walking along dreamily, his face illuminated by a smile, and his forehead aglow with joy and good humor as he quivered excitedly with love's intoxication. Didn't a lover's success provide pleasure and pride equivalent to a warrior's? He felt an irresistible desire to tempt him into a discussion of this beautiful subject. So gesturing toward the clumps of trees with a suggestive smile, he exclaimed, "Oh, if only these trees could talk!"

Ali Taha grasped the reference, and his sentiment was so vivid that he felt inspired to speak clearly, needing to express himself. So he said emotionally, "Mr. Mahgub, that's what you think, but don't cast a sarcastic eye on love. By no means. It should not be taken lightly. The throbbing of a serious heart is as significant in this world as the planets' trajectories are in the heavens. So don't ever mention the 'boiler's reservoir' or 'safety valve.'"

Mahgub felt profound contempt for his interlocutor. This was compounded both by the agitation his inflection betrayed and by the envy Mahgub felt for him. He told himself sarcastically: The idiot wants to fashion a shrine even for procreation. Then out loud, he said calmly and coldly, "You lovers, *I don't worship what you worship.*"

Ali smiled and responded in kind, *"Nor do we worship what you worship."*

Mahgub was afraid that his Qur'anic sarcasm would bring the young man back to his senses. He regretted his slip and wished to disguise it. So he changed his tone and said with superficial interest, "What a strange affair love is. Although your girlfriend really is exceptional!"

Ali replied enthusiastically, "Beauty's not her only virtue. Her spirit is refined, her heart is perceptive, and I can't begin to describe for you how perfectly our personalities mesh. This is Ihsan!"

Mahgub's soul was troubled by hearing her name and was suddenly filled with fury. Do you suppose this is the jealousy

44

that people discuss? How shameful! How could someone who aspired to smash all shackles fall victim to depraved jealousy?

In a different tone that masked his revived sarcasm, he shot back, "For this melding to be perfect, I suppose your girl must be liberated from religion and believe instead in society, high ideals, and socialism."

Ali replied primly, "It's enough for us to live a single emotional and spiritual life. Our two intellects will unite, commingling, so that we become a happy family one day."

Mahgub asked skeptically, "Have you reached that point?"

"Yes."

"Have you proposed to each other?"

"Yes. I'm waiting till she finishes her higher education."

"Congratulations, sir."

It hurt him to offer congratulations when he himself was the person who most deserved consolation. He was filled with anxiety and despair. He thought to himself: He beat me out of the prettiest girl in Cairo. Tomorrow the fresh, pliant body will belong to him. He blurted out a question without meaning to, "How did you meet her? On the street?"

Ali replied with astonishment, "Of course not! From the window!"

"But you're not the only one who looked down at her?" This sentence escaped without any premeditation as well. He deeply regretted uttering it and feared his companion would grasp its real meaning. So he added to mislead him, "Our student neighbors also look out."

Ali remained silent but smiled, and Mahgub did not say anything for fear his tongue would commit some new offense. They came in sight of the student hostel, which looked like a military barracks: a huge building with many small windows. They saw opposite it, at the corner of al-Izba Street, Uncle Shihata Turki's

45

home. The man, who was standing in front of his establishment, was in his fifties with a fair complexion and handsome face. Mahgub commented to himself sarcastically: What a great in-law he will be! Then the two young men entered the large structure: the happiest of men and the most wretched.

10

The three friends congregated in Ma'mun Radwan's room. The window was closed and the heater in the center of the room had a layer of ashes on top. Ma'mun was criticizing the Friday sermon he had heard that noon. He began by saying that sermons needed radical revision and that in their present state they were a frank incitement to ignorance and superstition.

His two companions paid no attention to sermons, but all the same, Ali Taha said, "The really pressing need is for preachers of a new type: from our college, not from al-Azhar. They would tell people that their rights have been plundered and show them how to liberate themselves."

Mahgub Abd al-Da'im customarily participated in his friends' discussions, not to defend one of his beliefs, because he did not have any, but from a love for contentious, mocking debate. This evening, though, more than ever, he felt he was one of those wretched people to whom Ali referred. He wanted to get some relief for the tightness in his chest by speaking. Although he was not concerned with the welfare of people in general, the only way he could refer to his own concerns was by couching them in universal terms. So he said, "Fine, our problem is poverty."

Then Ali Taha said fervently, "That's right. Poverty's fetid air stifles science, health, and virtue. Anyone who's content with the peasant's living conditions is a beast or a demon."

Mahgub added to himself: Or a bright guy like me, if that's the only way to get rich. Then out loud, he said, "We know the disease. That's obvious. But what's the cure?"

Ma'mun Radwan, adjusting his skullcap, said, "Religion. Islam's the balm for all our pains."

Stretching his legs out till they almost touched the heater and ignoring what his host had just said, Ali Taha replied, "The government and parliament."

So Mahgub objected, "'Government' implies rich folks and major families. The government is one big family. The ministers select deputies from their relatives. The deputies choose directors from a pool of relatives. Directors select department chiefs from relatives. Chiefs pick office workers from their relatives. Even janitors are chosen from among the servants in important homes. So the government is a single family or a single class of multiple families. And it's a fact that this class sacrifices the people's welfare whenever that conflicts with its own interests."

"How about parliament?"

Smiling mischievously, Mahgub answered, "A representative who spends hundreds of pounds to get elected can't represent impoverished people. Parliament's no different in this regard from any other organization. Look at Qasr al-Aini Hospital, for example. It's termed a hospital for the indigent, but actually it's a laboratory for potentially lethal experiments on the poor."

Ali Taha observed calmly, "Outrage is a sacred sentiment, but despair is an illness. In any event, parliament is a lake where separate streams meet. Inevitably these waters mix together and from them a new spring wells up."

Smiling bitterly, Mahgub muttered, "These are the names I admire: Ahmosis and the Hyksos, Merenptah and the Jews, Urabi and the Circassians!"

Ma'mun Radwan laughed and commented, "The strangest thing is that Taha's a constructive communist, but you're destructive. You, more than anyone, deserve the title anarchist."

Mahgub laughed so hard that he ended up coughing. He replied, "We impose far too much on ourselves—as if this room were responsible for the world's welfare."

Ali Taha said, "As long as it houses students, its walls will hear the hopes of successive generations."

Ma'mun Radwan observed attentively, "This room is an incubator. So what's next?"

Mahgub replied with malicious delight, "Prison—if any of us means what he says!"

Then, remembering the worries he had brought back with him from al-Qanatir, he lost his enthusiasm for debate. Rising, he excused himself, alleging that his trip had tired him. He went to his room, where he sat thinking sadly at his small desk. When January ended, his present "welfare" would end. Yes, this life had seemed an inferno to him in the past. Compared to what awaited him in the future, it would seem a lost paradise. There was no doubt that the next three months would bring forms of suffering he had never imagined. So what was he to do? He tugged on his left eyebrow, frowning, while determination and defiance flooded his pale face.

11

During the remaining days of January he busied himself searching for a cheap room. He had trouble, both because the neighborhood was heavily populated and because it was crowded with students who competed vigorously for isolated rooms on rooftops. Then, finally, he located a rooftop room in a new building on Jarkas Street, near Giza Square, but its newness proved a disaster for him when the building's owner refused to rent the room for less than forty piasters. Mahgub was forced to accept this rent unwillingly. He told his friends he would move to a room in a new building, informing them with a wink that special circumstances required it. He said that, even though he knew he would be unable to afford trysts with the cigarette butt collector in the future. All the same, he preferred a lie to humiliation. He found that he would need to pay for transportation and to purchase a kerosene lantern. Looking through his meager furnishings, he found nothing he could spare except his small wardrobe, which was more like a trunk than an armoire. With the concierge's assistance, he sold this secretly for thirty piasters. On the first of February, he bundled his possessions together, said goodbye to his friends, and moved to the new room. He paid the rent in advance, and then all he had left of his new allowance was sixty piasters, which had to last him the whole month: two piasters a day for food and kerosene, not to mention laundry—an unavoidable necessity. He could forget about paying a cleaner, and then there was shaving. As for his cup of coffee— that was a forbidden luxury. Among his miserable furnishings there was nothing he could spare or that would conceivably fetch a helpful price. His bed, which was his most important possession, was barely worth half a pound, whereas its utility was inestimable. He slept on top of it and stored his garments beneath it. He shook his head with its frizzy hair and mumbled, "The three months will pass like any others. I won't die of hunger at any rate." So he spent his first night in his new digs.

The next morning he left the room after closing everything. The concierge offered to clean it for him, but he rejected this offer with thanks. Actually he fled, because he could not sacrifice even a millieme to him. Reaching Giza Square, he cast his eyes around till they fell on a ful shop, which he glumly approached. He found groups of workmen seated on the curb in front of the shop devouring their food while talking and laughing among themselves. He told himself, "I've become one of these laborers Ali Taha pities." He ordered half a pita-bread stewed bean sandwich, which he ate with gusto after stepping aside. When he finished he was still hungry. By nature, he had a large appetite, and his normal breakfast was a plate of beans with a loaf of flat bread, not to mention an onion and some pickles, but now he could only eat two small snacks a day. Shrugging his shoulders, he headed toward the university, telling himself, "I desperately need to remain clearheaded, because either I succeed or kill myself." The school day passed as usual, and he met all his friends. They spent a considerable amount of time in the Orman Gardens discussing their lectures. When lunchtime arrived, he left them as they headed to the cafeteria. He returned to Giza Square. Only the day before, he had eaten in the cafeteria with Ali, Ma'mun, and Ahmad Badir. His lunch had been a plate of spinach with lamb and rice and then an orange. But today! As he approached the ful shop, the proprietor greeted him with a smile, saying "Welcome." This greeting hurt his feelings and deflated his pride. Next to the ful shop was a kebab stand, and the aroma of grilled meat wafted to his nostrils. He salivated and his stomach hurt. Then he took a complete pita bread sandwich, filled with ful midammis, and fled from the tantalizing scent. When he returned to his room and opened the door, the air smelled stale because he had left the window closed. Even so, he saw that dust covered his desk, his books, and his quilt, which lay on the bed. He realized that for the foreseeable future he would be a student, a servant, and perhaps a laundress, too. Vexed and rebellious, he set about his new tasks. This new life was hard and exhausting. He would doubtless continue with his studies. He would pursue them with stubborn determination, but hunger would not leave him alone and he would never feel rested. He lay awake nights, prey to hunger, or sat at his desk for long hours, his limbs frozen and his back bowed. His new circumstances might ruin his appearance and expose him to mockery and sarcasm. Perhaps hunger would debilitate and sicken him.

But he had no choice—he had to struggle stubbornly and obstinately. He was obliged to defy people, fortune, and the world at large. He had to become furious, to hate, and to fly off the handle. He kept working till midnight when he abandoned his desk for his bed. Lying down exhausted, he mumbled, "So ends the first night of my ordeal."

12

The next morning he woke up tired and headachy. Amazingly, he was not hungry, although he remembered his hunger pangs from the previous night, for the ful sandwich had not lasted him through the evening. Instead it had left in its wake an excruciatingly painful hunger. He thought about skipping breakfast so he could have a sandwich and a half for lunch. That would allow him to feel more comfortable during the evening and thus study with his mind at ease. During the first hours of the day, his courses would distract him from his stomach. This fine idea was appropriate for a poor, distraught head. He would rely on habituation to defang the pain. Nevertheless, he had barely taken a sip of water and inhaled the morning breezes on the street when his beastly stomach flexed its muscles, and his resolve broke down. So he hastened to the beanery, oblivious to anything else. While eating, he began to reflect on what people said about Hindu ascetics. He was amazed by their extraordinary ability to withstand hunger. How could they cope with this pain with such bitter patience and derive an elevated pleasure from the whole experience? Oh, my Lord! How this unique word "pleasure" varied according to human temperament! In his case, both pleasure and privation were clearly demarcated. Even the butt collector had become too precious to touch. He went to the faculty, attended his first class, and then went to the garden to wait for the second one, which began two hours later. He sat on a bench surrounded by a bunch of students who were basking in the sun's gentle rays, which February provided with a limited generosity. With youthful zeal, flitting from topic to topic as the spirit moved them, they discussed: the plump young woman whose volume was erratic and whose voice quavered when she rose to recite a text; Mr. Irving, the golden-haired Latin teacher, who should have been born a woman, whereas the brilliant young woman should have been a man; the cinema and how it threatened true culture and refined art; whiskey and hashish (which was more enjoyable); whether the 1923 constitution would be restored; who should be given more credit for founding the university (the king or the late Saad Zaghlul); whether members of the Young Egypt Association were sincere fellows or conspirators; who deserved more credit for the theater's resurgence (Yusuf Wahbi or Fatma Rushdi); and which would be better for the nation: that Prince Farouk should complete his studies in Italy, as his father wished, or in England, as the British wanted. Opinions and comments filled the air, which rang with laughter and shouts. Mahgub participated in the talk to some extent, listening cynically as usual to what was said. Then he rose and strolled through the vast garden. When it was just about time for class, he shot back to the faculty. Once that class was over, he left—arm-in-arm with Ahmad Badir.

The youthful journalist said, "Congratulations on your new digs."

Smiling, Mahgub replied, "Thanks."

Ahmad Badir asked, with a crafty smile, "From a good family or a good-time girl?"

Mahgub immediately grasped his companion's meaning and was relieved by it. With a mysterious smile, he replied, "This is a secret that cannot be disclosed."

"Does she live with you or come every night?"

Mahgub proclaimed proudly, "As you know, cohabitation courts suspicions."

The journalist nodded his head and puckered his lips. Then he exclaimed, "Lucky devil!"

As February's days passed and the cares of life beat him down, hunger's ghost haunted him night and day, because his stomach felt full for only limited moments. In addition to his schoolwork, he swept his room, cleaned his desk, made his bed, and washed his handkerchiefs, socks, and shirts. He did not know how to acquire necessities others would have considered a trivial expense whether a bar of soap, kerosene for the lamp, or the paper he needed. Some days he was forced to limit himself to one meal. Hunger ground him down. He grew ever leaner and his face more sallow, until he feared for his life, for his person, which he loved more than the whole world or which he loved even without loving the world. In a room that some of his friends thought a nest of fiery passion, he holed up, hungry and solitary. Why didn't he ask his brethren to feed him? Had he asked Ali Taha, that young man would not have hesitated or delayed. If he had asked Ma'mun Radwan, he would have shared his food with him, even if only a morsel of bread. What prevented him? A sense of honor? Pride? Damn that! Hadn't he spurned everything? Didn't he disparage all values? What were honor and pride to him? Damn it! His philosophy was still merely words and nonsense. When would he become a true man? When would he liberate himself from honor and reputation as if brushing dirt from his shoe?

His distress peaked when he was required to buy a Latin text that cost twenty-five piasters. He was dumbfounded. He did not even have a millieme he could devote to that, and the exam loomed ever nearer. What was he going to do? To ask one of his friends was an odious, hateful solution—especially since he knew he would never be able to repay the money. So what was he to do? One day after another passed as his life became ever more disturbed. He had almost given in to despair when he remembered his mother's distinguished relative—Ahmad Bey Hamdis. How could he despair when he had a notable relation like this? It was true that his father held a serious grudge against him, saying he was an ungrateful fellow who had forgotten his family and snubbed them. This was actually true, but his father was wrong to be angry. The bey's conduct was appropriate. If his relative put on airs, so did all men like him. They had a right to be uppity. The stupid rural moral code was solely responsible for his father's anger. Although the bey was conceited, that would not prevent him from viewing Mahgub's plight with an affectionate eye and from extending a helping hand. So he should seek out the bey in good conscience instead of loathing him.

13

He left his room, fully resolved to visit his relative and try his luck. He spared no expense in getting ready. He pressed his fez and shined his shoes for a whole piaster—in other words, the price of an entire meal. Even so, he looked like an invalid with a pale face and emaciated body. He looked up his relative's address in the telephone directory—al-Fustat Street in Zamalek—and hurried off.

On his way there, his imagination soared through a world of half-forgotten memories illuminating a distant period when he was eight and his relative was still Ahmad Effendi Hamdis, an engineer in al-Qanatir. The engineer's family consisted of his lovely wife, their daughter Tahiya, who was four, and a little boy of two. It was a happy family that drew strength from the exceptionally beautiful lady of the house. At that time the Hamdis family had not grown too important to exchange social visits with the Abd al-Da'im family, and Abd al-Da'im went all out to honor this dear family. How often he rushed to the markets to buy chickens and pigeons to prepare a tasty meal for them!

Mahgub himself had won the affection of Hamdis Bey's spouse, who praised his intelligence and admired his cleverness. She allowed Tahiya to play with him in the yard and the street. What would Tahiya be like now? Would she remember him? That era had been buried by fifteen years. It was forgotten, obliterated, and finished. Memories of it had been carried away by time and neglect. If they were of any significance, some trace of them must lie in a deep layer of memory. The Hamdis family, however, had ascended and become significant, whereas his family had remained as nondescript and insignificant as ever. Al-Qanatir had been erased from life's record and memories of it had sunk into the past's gloomy stretches. Abd al-Da'im Effendi, as a clerk in a Greek-owned firm, had been dismissed from mind. What was Tahiya like? Wasn't it possible she would remember him? That boy who carried her in his arms and ran with her from the house to the train station! Hamdis Bey could not have forgotten him; even if he had, he would remember him the moment he set eyes on him. He would not refuse to give him a hand.

He reached Zamalek and found his way—after asking for directions—to al-Fustat Street. Like Rashad Pasha Street, it was grand and still. On either side, towering trees were massed, and their branches met overhead, forming a canopy of red flowers. He cast an incredulous look at the mansions with his protruding eyes. This look seemed to ask, "Is it possible for suffering to penetrate these thick walls? Is what claimants to wisdom say true or do they enclose inflamed hearts?" With steady steps he approached the villa at number 14, where he asked the doorman in a refined accent and dignified tone for the bey, informing the man that he was a relative who had come to visit. So the Nubian doorman invited him into the parlor, and he entered a large, splendidly furnished chamber. He had never been in a house like this before or found himself in such a room. So he examined everything with a mixture of astonishment, admiration, and regret. Looking out a nearby window, he saw part of a garden that was filled with nature's fragrant beauties. How would the bey receive him? Would his wife invite him in so she could see what had become of the boy now that he was grown? Would they remember the time in al-Qanatir and ask affectionately about their old friend Abd al-Da'im Effendi? Would they be moved by his illness and discern the motive that had induced Mahgub to knock on their door and then extend a helping hand to him out of their good will? What a fine room! Wasn't it possible that he might own such a mansion that needy people would seek out?

Hearing footsteps, he looked toward the door. Then he saw the bey, whom he recognized at first glance, although his appearance had changed and he was older. As the bey approached, he rose and advanced toward him politely, extending his hand. They shook hands, and the bey scrutinized him. Then, smiling, the bey said, "So it's you! I didn't recognize the name at first, but then my memory came to my aid. Now you're a man. How are your parents?"

I didn't recognize the name at first! So it's you!

Mahgub overlooked all that and replied respectfully, "My mother's fine, but my father's ill. In fact, his condition is serious."

Then they sat down. The bey was wearing an overcoat. So it seemed he was preparing to leave the house. Leaning back in his chair, the man said, "I hope he'll recover. What's the matter?"

Mahgub said carefully and clearly, "My father had a stroke that has left him paralyzed in bed. He's had to quit his job and things are rough."

His hopes rested on this final phrase: things are rough. He stole a glance at the bey just after speaking but noticed no impact. Without any alteration in his glacial expression, the bey said, "That's too bad. I hope you'll give him my greetings. How about you, Mahgub—have you finished your studies?"

This change of topic infuriated him, and the speaker's coldness enraged him, but he felt obliged to answer, "My final-year exam is this May."

"Excellent . . . congratulations in advance."

Then he rose, saying, "I'm so sorry to leave you now, but I have an important appointment."

Full of despair and rage, the young man stood up, inwardly cursing a meeting that had lasted less than two minutes after a separation of fifteen years. Didn't the bey grasp the motive that had led him to his mansion? Hadn't the phrase "things are rough" suggested his reason for coming? With intense anxiety he followed the bey outside. He could grasp the bey's arm and yell at him, "I'm destitute and need your help. Give me a hand!" He was ready to spring into action, risking everything, when he saw a young woman and an adolescent boy calmly mounting the steps nearby. His resolve collapsed, and his look honed in on the approaching pair. He recognized Tahiya at first glance, in spite of the big difference between the beautiful image in front of him and the one in his memory. From the resemblance between her and the teenage boy he realized that this was her brother. He forgot his resolve and was aware both of floating in suspended animation and of his pride. The bey smiled at his children. Gesturing toward Mahgub, he said, "Mr. Mahgub, my relative . . . Tahiya, my daughter and her brother Fadil."

They shook hands. Smiling, Mahgub said, "I remember them clearly."

The bey, who was moving toward the automobile that awaited him, said, "In that case, stay and visit with them."

Should he? They exchanged curious, smiling glances. Fadil was a handsome youth of noble appearance. Mahgub hated him at first glance for his elegance, good looks, and nobility.

Tahiya was an extraordinarily beautiful girl. Ihsan Shihata's beauty might be more captivating, but Tahiya was a perfect model of elegance and pride, a living paragon of the aristocracy. She quickly dazzled his senses and he immediately discovered in her a vital symbol for the high society life to which his heart aspired. She set fire to his emotions and roused his ambition, even if she did not awaken his lust the way Ihsan did. She also did not awaken any lofty emotions in him, since he was unfamiliar with these. Instead his admiration for her was mixed with resentment, and his desire was blended with defiance. Deep inside he felt a longing to dominate and ravage her. He immediately decided to tarry with them. The three sat down in the magnificent parlor, and he felt certain that his shabby appearance was not lost on them. Even so, he felt only contempt for this fact, since he truly enjoyed an amazing ability to vanquish timidity and discomfort and to arm himself with boundless disdain.

Smiling, Fadil asked, "Do you really remember us, sir?"

Mahgub answered calmly, "We lived in the same town fifteen years ago when the bey was an engineer in al-Qanatir. We played together in our house's garden."

The youth said with astonishment, "I don't remember anything from that time!"

Tahiya commented in a voice as polished as her appearance, "It's almost the same for me."

That hurt him. Papering over his emotions with a smile, he said, "You were both young, but I was eight."

Nodding his head, the beaming Fadil asked, "Have you finished your studies?"

Was this question customary in aristocratic families? He answered, "I'll be done in May."

"Which faculty?"

"Humanities."

Fadil commented loftily, "We're happy to discover a relative like you."

Mahgub immediately responded, "I'm even happier because I've discovered two relatives."

Tahiya had been examining him with feminine eyes. Simply to make polite conversation she commented, "We haven't visited al-Qanatir since we left."

Uncharacteristically Mahgub felt at a loss. Should he invite them to visit al-Qanatir to see the house with its "garden" where they had played? Fadil, however, rescued him from his quandary by asking his sister sarcastically, "Have you visited Cairo, where you live? All you know are living rooms and the cinema."

Tahiya, blushing, smiled and retorted, "What a sarcastic exaggerater you are! Don't you realize that I know Cairo overall and have even visited the antiquities museum and the Pyramids like the tourists?"

An extraordinary idea occurred to Mahgub, who—on being released from his perplexity—immediately suggested, "The antiquities museum and the Pyramids are stale destinations. Have you visited the new excavations?"

Turning toward the speaker, Tahiya inquired, "New excavations?"

Pointing toward his chest as if personally responsible for the discoveries, he said, "The university's excavations—a few minutes' walk from the Pyramids—a strange world surrounded by barbed wire. All the people involved are my friends and colleagues. So when shall we go together to see them?"

Delighted, she replied, "I don't know, but I'll go some day. Isn't that so, Fadil?"

Fadil, who was beginning to feel listless, replied automatically, "Of course, of course."

Walking through the villa's garden after his visit, Mahgub Abd al-Da'im sensed that it was possible that a type of what people call friendship might grow between him and his two cousins. He wondered what he could get out of this friendship if it did arise—or would he emerge from it as empty-handed as from his visit with the bey?

14

He found himself once again on al-Fustat Street, buffeted by an unruly, cold wind which caught him by surprise. It shook the branches, making the street hum with their rustling. It blew past walls with a deafening whistle. A shudder passed through his enervated body and pervaded his joints; the month of Amshir was too harsh for a starving weakling to endure. Although distracted from his surroundings by his reflections, half conscious of the weather, he darted along the road. He thought of Fadil, comparing himself with the adolescent who enjoyed health, good looks, and wealth whereas Mahgub was ill, ugly, and poor. Nonetheless they were cousins! Tahiya was an aristocrat—a vibrant representative of the world he yearned for. Do you suppose he would ever take her to the Pyramids? A girl like her really was a magic key that could unlock doors and perform miracles. He brooded about this for a long time. But, alas! How could he sink into such dreams and forget his current concerns? How would he find the money to buy the book for Latin? How could he withstand his starvation diet that threatened his body and mind? How amazing! What greater proof of man's baseness was there than the need for food to sustain life? Could this food, which was extracted from clay and fertilized by garbage, constitute life's essence and mainstay? Was it thought's buttress? The true creator of ideals? Wasn't this proof that man's essence is vile rubbish? He quickened his steps. The winds kept on raging ferociously and the sky was overcast with dark clouds. The emerald waters of the Nile were roiled and turbulent. He cast an angry look at his surroundings and spat disdainfully on the ground as if to declare his enmity to the world. Shouldn't he borrow the money? From whom? How could he repay the debt? The next month would be no better than the previous one—in fact, it might be worse. What could he do? If only he knew how to pick pockets. There was a magical art! Pickpockets owned everything in anyone's pocket. The nation's rulers had grasped the significance of this insight. But what could he do? Should he renew his attack on Hamdis Bey? Should he meet him at his ministry and ask him point-blank for money? Tahiya's image disrupted this chain of thoughts—Tahiya with all her nobility and her aristocratic manners. Would he want her to learn he was a miserable beggar? This girl stirred his feelings, although he was not insane enough to rave the way Ali Taha did. This was a new passion. Like his passion for Ihsan, it was neither Platonic nor erotic. Amazingly, he felt enormously, incredibly self-confident, perhaps because of his native daring and audacity, not to mention the fact that—like the masses—he believed his sexual prowess outstripped that of the rich. He truly believed that Tahiya was not beyond his reach. The sky was not the limit for his dreams, which his hunger made even more fantastic, a hunger that turned studying into a bitter struggle and his nights into painful torture. The book for Latin? Damn it. How would he raise the money?

15

He felt calmer when he awoke the next day. The fantasies that his visit to the Hamdis family had aroused had died away. Thus he returned to his senses and decided that he should seek out Hamdis Bey at the ministry and present his request, even though this meant sacrificing his friendship with Tahiya and Fadil. He felt obliged to skip class and ate no breakfast so he would have enough money to ride the tram both ways. He set off at once, reaching the Ministry of Works at exactly 10 a.m. He learned the way to his relative's secretary, whom he found to be a man in his forties. He greeted him politely and told him, "I wish to see His Excellency the Bey."

"Who are you?"

"One of the bey's relatives—Mahgub Abd al-Da'im."

The man asked him to wait a moment and disappeared. Mahgub brooded about what he might say to the bey and how he should phrase his statement in the most moving fashion. The man returned shortly, sat down at his desk, and said, "The bey is chairing the Advisory Council; so it would be best for you to return another day."

This answer caught him off guard and upset him. He felt he had received a direct blow to the head. He implored the man, "But I want him for a very important matter."

"No doubt about that, but, God willing, some other day."

"I can wait an hour or two."

Then the man said in a tone that made it clear he wanted to extricate himself and move to something else, "Come in the evening if you want."

He left there enraged and infuriated. Should he let the tram gobble up his remaining money? No—to hell with the bey and his advisory council! He realized immediately that to save the cost of transportation he ought to wait downtown till afternoon if he wanted to see the bey. Since he could no longer resist the hunger that was wringing his stomach, he went to al-Azhar Square to search for a beanery. He took the food, on which he had subsisted for three weeks, and hurried to Qasr al-Nil Street to cool his heels in its gardens while he waited. The weather was cold and the sky overcast. He walked along with his head bowed, repeating resentfully and angrily, "The criminal humiliated me. The criminal humiliated me!" Nevertheless, he would need to chase after the man again. He was an enemy who must be befriended. The bey was simply another pain the world was using to test him. He passed his fingers over his fiery forehead and declared, "I won't cry . . . I'll keep a stiff upper lip. No matter how hungry I get, I won't scream like the cowards who call out, 'O Lord!'" His feet finally carried him to the garden where he began to split his time between sitting and walking in annoyed disgust. His limbs were cold and his stomach felt tired. In frightened alarm, he asked himself, "Isn't it possible that these black days will leave permanent scars?" His pale face frowned while sorrowful anxiety showed in his eyes. After waiting for half an hour, while he was walking on the road beside the Nile, not knowing where he would find the patience to wait for the appointment, he saw near the back gate of the Andalusian Garden two smiling girls, who were heading his way while chatting. Glancing casually at them he recognized that one of them was none other than Tahiya Hamdis. She did not notice him since her attention was focused on her companion. Coming upon her unexpectedly, however, had an overwhelming impact on Mahgub. His former train of thought was interrupted. He forgot her father and the advisory council. He turned a blind eye to his pains and hunger, because his attention was focused on one thing: meeting her. He could care less about his appearance and the presence of the girl he did not know. He kept his eyes on Tahiya, whose gray overcoat was draped around her with aristo-cratic elegance. Perhaps she sensed his gaze, because she glanced toward him when a few meters away. He stood right in front of her, bowing to greet her. Her face showed her astonishment and then she blushed. She glanced quickly at him and then offered him her hand. She introduced her friend, and then the three stood there somewhat awkwardly. He had been so keen to carry out his plan that he could think of nothing to say now and fell back on conventions of conversation, asking, "How is your family?"

She replied with natural grace, "They're fine, thanks."

Then his mind rescued him from his quandary, reminding him of the excavations. Delighted to have hit upon a conversation topic, he said, "This happy occasion gives me a chance to remind you that a free person keeps his promises."

Frowning in bewilderment, she said, "I don't understand."

In a censorious tone, he replied, "The excavations, the uni-versity's excavations."

"Oh . . . of course I haven't forgotten."

"When?"

"When!"

"Yes, let's be practical. What do you think about next Friday afternoon?"

She hesitated momentarily and then—since she liked the suggestion—said, "Fine."

"How about Fadil Bey?"

"I'll tell him."

"Let's set a time."

"We don't want to inconvenience you. So you name the time."

"Four p.m., in front of the bus station in Giza Square."

They said goodbye and parted. He continued on his way. This was a dazzling victory that surpassed all his expectations. The dream had turned into a date. Yes, he had noticed that her companion had scrutinized his appearance, but looks did not matter. Wasn't the most contemptible man one caught between two women? What if that man was Mahgub Abd al-Da'im! Probably their relationship would become stronger. This was no small affair, because Tahiya represented luck's compassionate arms that could raise lucky fellows on high. Moreover, she herself was precious and to be cherished. Who could say? All the same he realized that it was no longer possible for him to beg from Hamdis Bey. It simply did not make sense to beg from the father one day and have an affectionate and respectful meeting with his daughter the next. If he did that, the man would refuse to allow his daughter to accompany such a despicable young man, and out of self-respect she herself would refuse to go. The choice was between begging and meeting. But there was no longer any room for choice, or put another way he had already chosen without realizing it. That door had closed in his face. He found himself, after all the effort expended, wondering anxiously what he should do. "How can I get the cash?" He hurried along, perplexed and worried, his mind spinning ceaselessly. Then he remembered Mr. Salim al-Ikhshidi. His bulging eyes suddenly lit up. Yes, this former neighbor, who wasn't Ma'mun Radwan or Ali Taha—he wouldn't feel too embarrassed to ask him for assistance. Why shouldn't he look him up? What an idea! And the day was barely half over. The distance between him and the ministry would take half an hour at the most on foot. He should go there without any delay. So off he set.

16

He asked for the office of Mr. Salim al-Ikhshidi, secretary to Qasim Bey Fahmi, but was told, "No, he's office manager." They gave him directions. A tall, broad-shouldered office messenger with a luxuriant mustache stood at the door. He asked permission to enter from this man, who disappeared for a moment and then returned to say in a gruff voice, "Enter." Then he found a room packed with seated people, men and women. Al-Ikhshidi and his office were obscured by a half-circle of lower-ranking employees who were presenting their files. The young man looked at his surroundings and asked himself: When will this mass of humanity clear out? When would he get a chance to put in a word? Al-Ikhshidi's voice resounded through the room, and its tones rang with authority and power, as he commented, criticized, and chastised. The voices of his subalterns whined with explanation, interpretation, and apology. The subordinates eventually collected their files and left, one after the other, until the director was finished with them. Then he noticed the young man, offered him his hand,

71

and invited him to have a seat. Next he turned to the visitors, lit a cigarette, took a deep drag, and puffed out the smoke with pleased exhilaration. Delight and pride lit up his face while Mahgub stole some fleeting glances at him. He was smug and happy. Doubtless he had breakfasted on butter, cream, and honey. He looked healthy and contented in his large chair. Mahgub hated him and wondered sarcastically why he had not hung in his large office a picture of his revered mother—Umm Salim—in her black gallabiya soiled with straw. As usual the visitors came with special requests. Some presented pleas to be exempted from school fees, a lady asked for his help in advancing her son to the fifth level, a man asked that a relative be transferred to Cairo after spending twenty years serving in rural areas, and a young man asked permission to see the bey to present a composition about a child's life to the age of five. He heard all these people respectfully and deferentially refer to Salim as "Your Excellency," while he responded deliberately, haughtily, and arrogantly. Mahgub waited patiently with pained anxiety till this administrator had time for him. Then the miracle occurred, and the room was empty.

Al-Ikhshidi turned toward him and said, "This is how I spend my day. Then it resumes at night in the bey's mansion."

Mahgub wondered resentfully: Do you want me to pray to God to relieve you of your post? Then, smiling, he said flatteringly, "The more judicious a person is, the more judgments he's asked to make."

Al-Ikhshidi nodded his large head. He never tired of extolling his own grandeur and of mocking the merit of others. He was known for his sharp tongue and for attacking enemies and friends alike. It was truly said of him that he had constructed his life on the basis of continual labor, self-promotion, and slander of his competitors. His egoism, however, portrayed most of those in contact with him as competitors, and therefore only a few were spared his malice. He paid no attention to what was said of him, and it seemed he unconsciously preferred for people to call him atrocious rather than excellent. If some negative comment about him came to his attention, he would say disdainfully, "Everyone who loves truth is hated."

Nodding his large head, he told the young man, "I work nonstop, but has that protected me from people's slander? Far from it! Some people will never cease repeating that al-Ikhshidi advanced to the fifth level without spending even two years in the sixth."

Pretending to be incredulous, Mahgub said, "Was the merit promotion system devised to discount qualifications?"

"On the face of it I work in a ministry. The fact of the matter is that it's a dunghill. Now, my dear friend, what do you need?"

Mahgub swallowed, sat up straight, and then in a hopeful tone said, "Salim Bey, you're a former neighbor and a former classmate, and our refuge in difficult times. Your Excellency, my father is bedridden, and we're suffering. I'm in a desperate crisis. My money has run out. So allow me to ask you for some assistance."

Examining him with round eyes, Al-Ikhshidi saw he was ema-ciated. He had no training at all, however, in giving and no back-ground in charity. He was not one of those "weaklings" whose hearts are swayed by visible manifestations of misery. Thus he considered the young man and his wants a ridiculous impediment to his chain of thoughts. His first reaction was to act to eradicate this impediment. But what would be the appropriate thing to do? Should he apologize to the young man? He hated apologizing, especially to the powerless. Then, remembering something, he asked the youth, "Are you good in French and English?"

Mahgub felt disappointed. He had been expecting more than a pointless question. All the same, he replied, "Yes, I'm good at both."

"Excellent. Do you know the magazine *The Star*? The owner is my friend and classmate. He might welcome you as a favor to me."

"Would I translate some pieces?"

"Yes, articles . . . humorous pieces. Take my card to him. I'll speak with him about you by phone. You must excuse me now; I'm going to present my files to the bey. Isn't this the most honorable and expeditious solution for you?"

Al-Ikhshidi stood up, and—taking a file in his left hand—held out his right to the youth. Shaking hands, the miserable young man asked, "Does this kind of work pay well?"

Al-Ikhshidi laughed—Mahgub hated him intensely then—and said, "Perhaps you've heard about the wealth of journalists! It will be enough for you if your immediate needs are satisfied." Al-Ikhshidi preceded him to the door. Mahgub felt extremely apprehensive and was about to shout to request a few piasters, but the door opened before he could, and the office messenger's tall, burly body appeared. So he quit the room carrying away the card. He left the ministry gloomy and anxious, since his crisis was unresolved. *The Star* magazine, even if his initiative met with success, was a long-range solution. So what was he to do? How could he get hold of the cash? It was going on three p.m. and the weather was as cold as it had been that morning. He was walking along the street aimlessly, his mind clouded by despondency. The whole world had rejected him. Making a threatening fist, he said resentfully and angrily, in a voice that was almost a sob, "The whole world will pay for all my pains!" He had realized that his only hope was to ask Ali Taha and Ma'mun Radwan. He hated asking them but had no alternative now. The inevitable is inevitable. As he headed for the tram he wondered which would be better. Each of them was a noble young man, but he did not love Ali whereas he did not hate Ma'mun. Moreover, Ma'mun was a religious, God-fearing person who could be trusted to keep a secret, leaving it in the realm of mystery. He would most likely be forbearing if he was late in repaying his debt.

He went to the hostel and headed for Ma'mun Radwan's room. The young man welcomed him with delight and asked, "Why did you skip class today?"

Mahgub replied, "Bad stuff, brother. I'm really in a bind."

With his large, black eyes, Ma'mun examined his face and was alarmed by how emaciated and despondent it looked. He asked with concern and compassion, "What's wrong, Mr. Mahgub?"

Without beating around the bush, he replied, "Rough times. I've lost my last millieme. I don't have even a millieme to buy the text for Latin."

Ma'mun stood up without uttering a word, went to the clothes rack, thrust his hand into the pocket of his jacket, and took out three ten-piaster bills, which he handed to the young man. Incredulous, Mahgub took them. He opened his mouth to thank his friend, but Ma'mun hastily put a finger to his lips, mumbling, "Hush."

Mahgub left the hostel, oblivious to everything. He did not even give a fleeting glance to Ihsan's house. He was both pleased and furious; pleased at obtaining the money and furious that he was indebted to Ma'mun Radwan.

17

he day for the Friday rendezvous arrived, and he went to the bus station shortly before the appointed time, wondering whether they would be true to their word. A magnificent automobile pulled up in front of the station right on time, and the beautiful face peered out of the window. His heart pounded and he hastened toward her. A door was opened for him and he took his place. Only then did he realize that Tahiya had come alone. He was amazed by that, but his amazement did not last long, because an all-encompassing delight overwhelmed him. Even so he asked with mock disapproval, "Where's Fadil Bey?"

The girl ordered the chauffeur to drive on. Then she turned to Mahgub and said in a critical tone, "We set out together, but on the way he saw 'some people' and renounced the trip, leaving me to make his apologies to you."

Mahgub looked down to hide his delight. He asked politely, "How are your excellent parents?"

"Praise God . . . they thank you for this lovely excursion."

"It's nothing, really."

In an expectant voice she said, "We'll see amazing things, isn't that so?"

Although he was going there for the first time, he assured her, "Absolutely."

Then they were silent. The girl was looking out the window, and he began to peer at her stealthily. This was the first time he had ever been alone with a female who really deserved to be described as feminine. And where were they? In a magnificent automobile that would "turn people green with envy"—he preferred that expression to saying, "turn heads." His nostrils were intoxicated by a sweet fragrance—instead of the smell of sweat encased in dirt. He could have been a man gasping for air who is brought into room pumped full of oxygen. He had not an iota of preparation for the creation of pure, celestial images. Thus his desire was channeled into one representation: that of throwing himself upon her. He felt his lust beginning to pulse through his blood. Looking outside, he wondered what had detained Fadil. Had he seen a pretty girl and chased after her? Or, had Tahiya herself contrived to get rid of him? His sexual conceit beguiled him. So he told himself that he and she were of one blood and that, as they say, "Blood creates sympathy." Nothing was impossible. He told himself: If intuition can be trusted, you'll see delightful things to your heart's content. The chauffeur? He doesn't count.

He couldn't imagine that one and the same person could be both rich and chaste. "No doubt these drivers are trained to turn a blind eye. Yes, yes—why else would she have come alone?" An exceptionally beautiful maxim states, "When a man is alone with a woman, Satan is also present." Where was Satan so he could bow and kiss his feet? He had long followed the devil as his disciple; wouldn't the devil reward him affectionately for his loyalty? He moved his eyes back inside and felt moved to draw her into conversation. So he asked, "Are you at the university?"

She shook her head no and said with a smile, "Banat al-Ashraf College."

He said delightedly, "Marvelous . . . marvelous."

Tahiya asked him, "What do you plan to do once you've earned your degree?"

Her question caught him off guard. His contemporaries spoke of the future with sorrow and despair. Recent graduates hunched behind desks in ministries, where they used their diplomas to fan brows made feverish by the humiliation of government service at the eighth level. With typical audacity, however, he freed himself from his bewilderment and replied with confident certainty, even though he knew he was lying, "I'll have to choose one of two paths: either entering diplomatic service or continuing on to a Ph.D. and teaching at the university."

"Marvelous," she commented, smiling.

Why did she use the same word he had? Was this she-devil mocking him or did she know nothing about such matters? Wishing to sound her out, he asked, "Which would you prefer?"

"Me? This is your concern."

With shrewd cunning, he explained, "It concerns you too, since we're related."

Blushing, she said, "Diplomacy is nicer."

He pictured Hamdis Bey going to the Ministry of Foreign Affairs to recommend his appointment. Then he said, "That's what I think. How beautiful it would be to spend one's whole life stationed in Brussels, Paris, and Vienna."

She giggled and asked, "Or in Damascus, Ankara, and Addis Ababa?"

He laughed along with her but added cleverly, "These are not capitals to which a relative of Hamdis Bey would be posted."

They both smiled. He told himself contentedly that a discerning person grasps indirect allusions; and that sufficed for him at the moment. As for the future, his heart told him that this girl would never disappear from his life without a trace. Who could say? He did not lack boldness; indeed, perhaps he was too bold for his own good. He surrendered to the stream of his thoughts until he saw that the automobile was climbing the twisting road to the Pyramids Plateau. They left the car at the foot of the Great Pyramid.

He said, "The excavations are some distance beyond the Sphinx."

They set off on a daunting path where their feet began to sink into the sand to be extracted only with some effort. It was late afternoon and the weather was cold even though the sky was clear and the sun shone down unveiled. By the light of day his clothes did not look elegant or attractive. He felt nervous and told himself sarcastically: Perhaps she's wondering why his Excellency the Ambassador isn't wearing a jacket. After walking for twenty minutes, they caught sight of the excavations, which were surrounded by a barbed wire fence. Then Mahgub stammered, "Here we are."

The young man went up to the watchman, whom he dispatched with a note to the superintendent. The guard soon returned and admitted them. Then the inspector, who was a young man in his twenties, came. He was a friend of Mahgub's and welcomed them warmly. He explained apologetically, "You'll see the areas where visitors are allowed. These are where digging has finished, but I can't accompany you because I'm really busy right now, and I don't think you need a guide." Mahgub nodded his head in agreement. "Fine. Here's the Temple of the Sun. It's part of the ancient temple complex known as the Temple of the Sphinx. Adjoining it is part of the rear section of the tomb of Prince Sennefer."

Mahgub told himself: God has ordained, for a reason He alone knows, that I be alone with her today. If all of God's wisdom is on a par with this, then I'm a believer! He escorted his precious treasure to the Temple of the Sun. They descended some recently constructed steps and found themselves in a granite-floored chamber with a row of columns on each side. There was no ceiling and nothing to astonish or excite a person's amazement. The girl cast a disinterested glance around her, and Mahgub was no less disappointed. Determined to extol the importance of this excursion, however, he said, "Look at these columns and how they have withstood the ages!"

She smiled—almost sneering—and replied, "What difference would it have made if they had been obliterated?"

Pointing to the carvings on the columns, he said, "If we could read the hieroglyphics, we would learn astonishing things."

"Really!"

"Certainly. Don't you know pharaonic history?"

She shook her head no. Thus the first part of the visit came to an end. As they approached the tomb behind the temple, Tahiya asked, "Aren't there other ruins besides this tomb?"

Sensing the boredom that prompted this inquiry, Mahgub felt nonplussed and answered, "There are many ruins, but we aren't allowed to visit the others."

Descending some steps, they found themselves in a long, narrow room the walls of which were decorated with carvings and frescoes. Their heads almost touched the ceiling. They cast a look around. Then the young man fixated on the frescoes and said in a faint voice, "Let's look at the pictures. See how brilliant the colors are."

They began near the entrance with the wall where the beneficiary of the tomb was portrayed with his wife on his left and their children between them. They were surrounded by servants and retainers. In the following panel they saw a picture of an expansive field that was being cultivated by oxen pulling plows. Standing here and there were naked peasants. Tahiya spent hardly any time at all on this image and moved on to the third panel.

Mahgub realized that the pictures of naked people embarrassed her. As he examined these images with bulging eyes, a malicious smile spread across his lips. His heart beat faster, and he sensed even more strongly their isolation. He did not leave the picture of the field and did not turn his eyes away from the representations of naked people. Thus his soul was filled with this extraordinary reality: that they were alone together in front of naked people. He gazed so assiduously that he imagined the figures were becoming three-dimensional before his eyes and starting to throb with life as blood flowed through their veins, their bodies were washed with an incandescent reddish hue, and fleeting glances flashed in their eyes. Then their necks craned toward . . . the fleeing girl, whose cheeks were crimson from embarrassment. His heart pounded violently, and his limbs were inflamed by his strong emotion. He tried in vain to control himself. He remembered that she had come alone and recalled their conversation in the automobile, her affability, their isolation, and their presence in this tomb, which enveloped them with a centuries-old savagery. He imagined that the fruit was ready to pick, and his inner tur-moil bubbled up until he became a savage beast deficient in both mind and volition. He swallowed, making a weird sound. His eyes were fixed on the naked figures, even though he no longer saw anything. He asked, "Haven't you looked at this field that's full of . . . ."

She retorted tersely in a way that suggested boredom, "There's nothing worth seeing."

He turned his head and almost whispered, "How easily bored you are, Miss."

He moved closer to her till he was beside her. Then he began to study along with her a picture of a servant kneading bread. He leaned over a little as if to inspect a detail of the picture, brushing against her shoulder and right hand. Then straightening again, he looked into her eyes and said in a quavering voice, "Don't you like anything?"

She laughed delicately and replied frankly, "The fact is that we haven't found anything to justify the trip."

In a shaky voice, his eyes piercing hers, Mahgub said, "But the place is beautiful and calm. . . ."

She noticed his trembling voice and sensed his intense, fiery gaze. Then her eyes twitched and she looked down. Frowning anxiously, she said, "It's time for us to leave."

He nodded his head and tried to say something but found he could not speak. So he seized her hand, which she quickly took back, gazing at him with disgust. He paid no attention to this, took her hand again by force, and said—as emotion swept like a wave over the surface of his visage, "Let's stay a little longer." The devil of desire seized control of him. So he pressed her to him violently and put his arms around her. His mouth, which was burning to devour her, descended toward her. She, however, fended him off with her right hand and pulled her head away from him. Anger flared in her beautiful face, and she shouted at him in a voice that echoed disturbingly in the silent tomb, "You're crazy! Let me go! Let go of my hand!"

Almost insane with torment, he pleaded with her, "Don't be angry . . . I beg you . . . come to me."

She broke free of his arms, however, with a wild force she did not know she possessed and shouted with stern determination, "Stay where you are! Don't you dare touch me. Don't you try to stop me."

She headed for the door. He yielded and followed her, his head bowed, silent, weighed down by feelings of shame and embarrassment. They walked along silently, retracing the route they had traversed as happy friends. Her beautiful face was overcast by an angry dark red. She held her head high with pride and conceit. He did not know how to atone for his error. The longer the silence lasted, the more desperate and defeated he felt, as he wondered regretfully if he should have been more patient. He told himself sadly: Obviously a girl like Tahiya shouldn't be treated like the butt collector. Perhaps he had not allocated to Tahiya a due amount of suave courtship. If only he had employed more deliberation and patience with her, he might well have succeeded. Damn unruly passion! It had cost him an auspicious opportunity.

When they reached the automobile, without glancing at him, Tahiya commanded, "Stay where you are!"

She climbed into the car, closed the door, and ordered the chauffeur to depart. He followed her with his eyes until she was lost from sight as the automobile quit the Pyramids Plateau, leaving him alone. He stayed where he was for a time—just as she had ordered—feeling gloomy. Then he shrugged his shoulders. As the spirit of contempt returned, he almost laughed at himself. He looked at the pyramid for a long time. Then he muttered sarcastically, "Forty centuries have watched my tragedy from the top of this pyramid." A sudden wave of anger overwhelmed him, his pale face turned red, and his nostrils quivered. He felt like pelting Cairo with huge stones from the pyramids. His feet started moving, even though anger still devoured him. Why was he sad? She was just a female and no better than his girlfriend, the butt collector. Right. All the same, he had blown an opportunity, losing Tahiya and her father forever. He thought for a moment. Then, shrugging his shoulders, he murmured contemptuously, "Tuzz."

18

A period of relative stability ensued.

Mahgub put his failure behind him and set to work enthusiastically. He met the editor of *The Star* and was commissioned to translate some pieces at a rate of fifty piasters a month. So his income rose to a pound fifty, and this sufficed to ward off the prospect of starving to death. It rendered his life tolerable at any rate. He began to work nonstop, night and day, at both his university studies and his undemanding journalistic chores. He had no free time and thus rarely thought about himself or ruminated about his afflictions. Whole days passed when he did not clench his fist in anger or yell "Tuzz!" with sardonic fury. Yes, he experienced a few brief moments of inevitable rage when he prepared to consume his vile food, for example, when he saw Ali Taha's athletic body and happy smile, or when he remembered knocking on doors to beg for a few piasters. Except for these occasions, life proceeded with tolerable comfort.

March passed with its mild weather, fine winds, and a sky that was beginning to shed its winter cloak to welcome spring's heat and fragrance. Next came April with its sun—as jaunty as any other upstart—and its dust-laden winds and bilious, grimy weather. His father's usual monthly letter arrived at the beginning of May. In it he said he was sending the last pound note he could spare. He prayed for his son's good fortune and success. Then he added that he was expecting his son's support, which he so badly needed, from that time forward. He included the good news that, God willing, he would soon be able to move and perhaps even to walk with a cane. There was nothing in the letter they had not already agreed on, but Mahgub could not repress the rage that shook him as he remembered his black nights—nights when he was starving and delirious. He kept saying of his parents, "If only they had been . . . I would have been. . . . If only they had been . . . I would have been. . . ."

Then the examination came on the first of May, and the results were announced by the twentieth. The four friends, who had been classmates for four full years, all passed. The examination was for Mahgub not merely an academic exercise. As a matter of fact, it was his one and only opportunity to reap the reward for fifteen years of effort. So he was doubly delighted, breathing a huge sigh of relief. A graduate's delight with his success is, however, brief. Indeed, it is a joy that lasts merely through the night the results appear. The next morning, especially if his circumstances resemble Mahgub's, he is burdened by concerns of a new type—those of a young person whose student's cloak has been shed only to confront alone the veiled tyrant, which brings opportunities for happiness and pitfalls threatening misery, called the future. The companions began to meet almost every evening at the university club where news reached them of classmates—with connections and family influence—for whom the doors of government service had opened. The four friends discussed their futures with positive comments and criticism, both optimistic and pessimistic. Ahmad Badir was wont to say contentedly, "My life's plan isn't going to change, because I'm not searching for a new career. Yesterday I was a student and a journalist. Now I can concentrate on journalism."

Ma'mun Radwan did not know whether he would be sent to France or would stay in Egypt, but his objective, which was Islam, remained the same in either case. He once asked, "Couldn't we start our real struggle with a Young Muslims Association? We would purify Islam of all the dusty pagan practices and reclaim its youthful spirit. We would broadcast our appeal across the entire Arab East before blanketing all Muslim lands." Ali Taha's objectives were unclear, and he seemed confused about how to achieve any of them. He was ready to get involved with politics, but only under the kind of political system that appealed to him, not with what was currently available. If he could find a party with progressive social principles, he would join without hesitation, but where was such a party? Should he wait for parties of this type to arise before entering politics or should he take the initiative now? It was doubtless easier to wait and also more judicious, since what use was there in advocating social reform in a country that was preoccupied by its constitution and pact with Great Britain. Perhaps it would be better to wait a little till he stockpiled more knowledge and information, and so on. He had not set his heart on a career appointment but also would not turn one down if it were offered.

Only Mahgub Abd al-Da'im was panic-stricken. Islam, politics, and social reform were topics that did not interest him. His sole concern was fending off death by starvation and that meant a job that paid a living wage. If he failed to find work, starvation threatened not only him this time but his parents as well. He was less concerned about them than about the awkward position in which they had placed him. What could he do? There actually was no patron who would help him, and no one received a government position without such support. He thought for a long time but did nothing more than write to tell his father that he was about to look for work and that he hoped to be able to fulfill his duty toward his family soon. He explained the difficulties he faced. Then the French professor of philosophy nominated Ma'mun Radwan for a fellowship at the Sorbonne and also recommended Ali Taha for an appointment at the university library, where he would find a suitable atmosphere for preparing an MA thesis. On hearing this, Mahgub compared his luck to his comrades'. Soon Ma'mun, child of the most miserable village in al-Gharbiya Province, would move to Paris. Soon Ali would settle comfortably into his chair at the library, preparing his thesis and announcing his engagement to Ihsan. Bravo, bravo! What was he doing? Would the black days of February return? He went to meet Ali Taha at the library a week after his appointment, expecting to find him overjoyed. The young man greeted him with his customary smile, but Mahgub did not detect in his expression the joy he had anticipated. Indeed, he imagined he saw instead an unfamiliar languor. He was totally amazed and so perplexed by this that he suspected the young man was attempting to hide his happiness behind the mask of listlessness. They talked at length, and Ali announced his intention to leave the position.

He said, "This is a time for me to wait and think while I discover a way to enter public affairs. Perhaps I'll choose journalism when the moment is right."

Mahgub was reminded of his work at *The Star* and of the vast wealth it showered on him. A sarcastic smile spread across his lips. Then Ali Taha continued, "I'm preparing to write a study of the distribution of wealth in Egypt."

Crushed by his friend's expectations, Mahgub asked bluntly if there was any possibility he could find a job at the library. The young man took him to the personnel officer to ask his opinion.

The man was very blunt. He took Mahgub's hand and told him sharply, "Listen, son. Forget your qualifications. Don't waste money on applying for a job. The question boils down to one thing: Do you have someone who will intercede for you? Are you related to someone in a position of power? Can you become engaged to the daughter of someone in the government? If you say yes, then accept my congratulations in advance. If you say no, then direct your energies elsewhere."

He left the library, his eyes clouded by despair and failure's bitter taste. What he had heard wasn't news to him. All the same, it infuriated him as if he were hearing it for the first time. Gloomy and despairing, he proceeded to stomp around the Orman Gardens. Oh, if only he had stayed on good terms with the Hamdis family! If only he had not ended that relationship by acting like a barbarian that day at the pyramids! Why couldn't he ever do anything right? Why couldn't he grasp his share of happiness and satisfaction? Why should hunger stalk him as if it could find no other prey? The world as a whole was happily ignoring him. Spring pulsed through the green boughs and crimson blossoms, flew high with the sparrows and larger birds, and danced on the red lips that were busy speaking to his right and left. The entire world was happy and blissful. Faces beamed. The Orman Gardens were a collage of human, animal, and plant delights. The earth itself and the sky were enveloped by a silent rapture surpassing any words. Would he starve to death in such a world? The question seemed bizarrely eccentric to him. He laughed mockingly, sarcastically, defiantly. He asked rebelliously, "Should I die of hunger? May rain never fall. May rain never fall." How could he starve to death while rejecting conscience, chastity, religion, patriotism, and virtue too? Had anyone who was really depraved gone hungry in this world? No, weren't they accused instead of appropriating all the good things in life? Why shouldn't he print a classified ad in *al-Ahram* saying, "Young man of twenty-four with university degree, ready to undertake any job no matter how depraved. With a clear conscience, he will sully his honor, chastity, and conscience in exchange for seeing his ambitions satisfied." Wouldn't prominent figures fight for his services? But who would publish such an announcement for him? Who would take him by the hand? It was no use running to his former classmates, his professors, or to Hamdis Bey. There was only one person left, and that was Salim al-Ikhshidi, who was neither chivalrous not benevolent. But who else was there?

19

He thought it best to visit al-Ikhshidi at home, because his office at the ministry did not offer a calm enough environment. So he went to al-Munira, where the gentleman occupied an apartment on al-Sayyid al-Mifdal Street, choosing Friday morning to assure he would be home. The gent, who lived alone in Cairo, cared for by a cook, received him in a small but elegant parlor. The host intuitively grasped the motive for the call but nonchalantly allowed his visitor to make his request.

Mahgub said, "I apologize for coming to your home, but I know your work in the ministry does not allow you to hear private concerns."

Al-Ikhshidi replied coldly, "I actually work all the time except for a brief period on Friday."

Mahgub grasped the veiled criticism but with customary boldness chose to ignore it, saying, "I've been awarded my degree."

Al-Ikhshidi smiled in languid encouragement and mumbled, "Congratulations."

The young man thanked him enthusiastically and continued, "Salim Bey, you are a former neighbor and classmate, our guide in both learning and patriotism. So long as I live I'll never forget that you saved my life and my future by introducing me to the editor at *The Star*. That's why I've come to you with a big request. Your Excellency, a degree without a patron is less valuable that wrapping paper. Could you possibly direct me toward some position?"

Al-Ikhshidi listened impassively, since he was used to hearing impassioned speeches like this. He despised the young man and scorned his poverty and need. He did not feel much like helping him. There were two vacant positions at the ministry, but he had promised one to an individual and had received a magnificent present with reference to the other. Mahgub might come in handy some day, but a quick fix was preferable to one long-delayed. Mahgub began to gaze at him with eyes full of fear and hope. He sensed that he was at the mercy of an egoist. Receiving no response, he said touchingly, "I've taken too much of your time."

Then al-Ikhshidi lit a cigarette and nodded his head as if he were sorry, even though his eyes remained expressionless. He observed calmly, "We have no positions vacant at the moment."

Despair swept over the face of the young man, who asked, "Is there any hope?"

"There's no need for total despair. We don't have any positions, but there are many elsewhere in the government; I might be able to steer you in the right direction."

There was nothing particularly encouraging about this remark, but Mahgub felt compelled to respond, "Thank you, bey. Thank you."

Al-Ikhshidi gave him a very enigmatic look and said, "I hope you'll be pragmatic, grasp how the world works, and learn that every favor has a price. I'm not asking for anything myself, because I'm simply a guide."

"Don't say that. I beg God's forgiveness."

Al-Ikhshidi smiled and replied, "If you catch my drift, there are capable people who can help individuals like you."

Al-Ikhshidi was silent for some moments before he continued, "There's Abd al-Aziz Bey Radwan, for example. Haven't you heard of him?"

"Of course. I think he's a well-known businessman."

"So he is, and currently his word carries a lot of weight. His sphere of influence is the Ministry of the Interior."

The young man asked anxiously, "Why would he help me?"

"The way is easy, but you ought to know his cut from his nominees is a guarantee of half of the salary for a period of two years."

This price alarmed the devastated young man. He looked at his companion fearfully. Then after some hesitation, he asked, "Isn't there someone less demanding?"

Like a waiter reciting a menu, al-Ikhshidi immediately replied, "The well-known musician Miss Dawlat."

Astonishment showed on the young man's pale face. The other man ignored his reaction and continued, "Her area of influence is the railways, Ministry of Defense, and some of the larger agencies."

Al-Ikhshidi drew heavily on his cigarette and then added, "The prices are as follows: eighth level: thirty pounds; seventh: forty; sixth: one hundred . . . payable in advance."

Mahgub sighed in despair. Then after reflecting briefly, he said, "I suppose Abd al-Aziz Bey Radwan's condition is more realistic, since I don't have even a millieme of the sum requested by the musician. I could relinquish half of my salary if I had one. How do I contact him?"

"You can't now—not for a month and a half, when he returns from performing the pilgrimage."

Damn him! Mahgub would starve to death before the man returned. In a faint voice, as though afraid of vexing his companion, he observed, "Waiting means starvation, but what can I do?"

Laughing for the first time, al-Ikhshidi said, "You're not a toy boy and your mother's not a flirtatious coquette. So what can I do?"

They were silent, and al-Ikhshidi would certainly have ended the meeting had something not occurred to him. He considered quickly and then assured himself that while Mahgub would prob-ably benefit from the experience, he himself certainly would—if his plan succeeded. So he said, "There's Mrs. Ikram Nayruz."

"Founder of the Society for Blind Women?"

"Yes."

"But she's very wealthy—her fortune's proverbial."

"Yes, yes. The lady doesn't ask for money but is fond of fame and praise. I could introduce you to her some time. Then it would be up to you, relying on your pen and *The Star*. Should you succeed in pleasing her, your future will be guaranteed. She has vast influence in many ministries and political parties."

He was hoping to exploit the young man to do publicity for her after introducing him as one of his flunkies. So he said, "Mrs. Nayruz is hosting a benefit next Sunday at the Society for Blind Women. Attend the party, and I'll introduce you to the lady. Write about the benefit and its patron, and we'll see . . . we'll wait and see."

"Will I achieve my objective this way?"

"That depends on your pen! You'll have to purchase a ticket for fifty piasters, since you're not a card-carrying journalist. Hopefully you'll realize later that this trivial sum has been of more utility than sixty pounds paid to Miss Dawlat. So get with it. Don't delay."

Despite his daring, when it came to borrowing the price of admission from his coach, his courage failed him. So he stood up, shook the man's hand gratefully, and left.

93

20

ifty piasters! The sum truly was insignificant, but how was he going to get hold of it? He had actually earmarked his desk and books to sell to support him during the month before his first paycheck. Do you suppose he would ever receive this salary? Who would give him the price of the ticket? Ma'mun Radwan had gone to Tanta to say goodbye to his family before leaving for Europe. So that only left Ali Taha. What was inevitable was inevitable.

He went to the university library Saturday morning, and Ali Taha greeted him with his customary smile, but Mahgub saw at first glance that his friend was feeling sad. This was not the Ali Taha he knew; the brilliant light of his eyes had gone out. His vivacious, energetic spirit had died. All of this might have delighted Mahgub in other circumstances. Today, however, he was worried that this sorrow might prove a stumbling block for his visit's objective. Pretending not to notice his friend's expression, he asked, "How's your study coming?"

Ali Taha swelled with vexation and replied with palpable despair, "I don't know. I can't do anything now."

Mahgub frowned, pretending to sympathize. Secretly cursing his inescapable bad luck, he said, "May God suppress this evil. What are you talking about?"

Ali had a nervous temperament and could barely conceal his secret. So he said, "As you might guess, it concerns Ihsan!"

Cold water might as well have been splashed on Mahgub's face. His interest aroused, he stammered inquisitively, "Your fiancée?"

"My fiancée," Ali sighed with brokenhearted grief.

Mahgub's astonishment increased. He commented as if wanting to know everything, "I don't understand at all."

Ali hesitated for a second. Should he reveal his secret? He was not secretive by nature and Mahgub was a friend with whom he had shared the story of his love. Moreover he badly needed to talk about it. So in a voice that clearly revealed his deep affliction and despair, he said, "I don't either. I can't tell you how dumbfounded and perplexed I've been. I keep asking myself: What happened? What wretched, furtive motives exuded their poisons in the dark? Life was proceeding beautifully. We were in love, and our love increased over time. We understood each other and grew closer as the days passed. We knew our past and appreciated it. We were conscious of our present and were satisfied with it. We had hopes for our future and looked forward to it. We met repeatedly and felt perfectly comfortable with each other. Our affection sank deep roots."

He fell silent for a moment. His companion's eyes never left his gloomy face. Then, enchanted by the fervor of the conversation, he burst out, "What spoiled our life? It's incredible, but that's the unvarnished truth. How did this occur? She began to change. At first the change was slight, but it didn't escape my wakeful, vigilant heart. I detected an anxious, perplexed look in her eyes.

She was absentminded at times, and her smiles grew lukewarm. She began to avoid talk about love. She was on guard against any mention of our hopes and promises. I privately vowed to be patient for a time, although I felt bitter anxiety and painful doubt. But this was to no avail, because nothing changed. I shared my suspicions with her, telling her that our love was worth nothing if she kept secrets from me. But she accused me of exaggerating and apologized for any change by referring to her indispositions. So my torment and pain doubled. How could I believe that a love like ours would suddenly die, without any warning? I longed for her but our meetings became a living hell. Finally she broke up with me. Can you believe that? I went crazy, stalking her. I sent her letters and persevered stubbornly, pursuing her. So she agreed to meet me. She arrived shattered by sorrow and shame. I shouted at her that her changes would drive me insane."

The young man ceased speaking. Mahgub had been following him intently, hanging on his words with such interest that he nearly forgot why he had come. He pretended to be deeply moved in order to encourage his friend to continue speaking.

Ali said, "I told her that her transformation would drive me insane. Then she said that meeting me really did drive her crazy. She told me that our hopes were destined to expire and that we should tend our sorrow sagely, satisfying ourselves with the inevitable conclusion. Should I agree to suffer without any attempt to defend myself? Should I forsake my happiness without asking why? She told me that it was her parents' desire and that she had given up attempting to change their minds after trying everything possible. She finally begged me to withdraw so I wouldn't add to her suffering."

The young man looked at Mahgub for a long time till he lost some of the intoxication of his recital. Then he blushed and asked,

"Why am I boring you? Everything's over. My hopes are shattered. Studying wisdom is pointless."

Mahgub was totally amazed. Why would Uncle Shihata Turki, a cigarette vendor, reject Mr. Ali Taha? Did he think the young man wasn't fit to marry into his family? Or did the man want his daughter to finish her studies and support his family? Then something occurred to him. He asked his friend, "Isn't it possible that some rich and prominent fellow wants the girl and her father would like to marry her to him?"

Ali raised his eyebrows anxiously but said nothing. Remembering the original goal of his visit, Mahgub now wished to pave the way for it. Ali's confession delighted his soul, which felt energized and joyful. All the same, he told his friend, employing a preacher's jargon, "In any event, you shouldn't surrender to sorrow. I tell you that no matter what the true motive for this rupture was, your girl no doubt played some role. So consider her something that never existed and toss the whole affair—cause and effect—into the wastebasket."

Ali protested sorrowfully, "The wound hasn't healed yet!"

"This is what you get for yielding to your theory about love. Don't you see that dogs deal with love in a way that's more conducive to happiness and contentment? We're always responsible for our own suffering."

Ali remained silent. So the preacher continued, "Forgetfulness . . . forgetfulness. Do you want to turn into one of those maniacs whose lives were ruined by love?"

Silence prevailed. A powerful reason for him to loathe Ali Taha had now been erased. He no longer hated him the way he had. The weight of his aversion was lightened and he began to ask himself: What harm does it do him to lose Ihsan? He still has his job, youth, and good looks. Since Ihsan had long set Mahgub's emotions on fire, it was a relief that his rival had not won her—even if a third party had. He stood up, preparing to obtain what he wanted. Leaning toward his friend as they shook hands, he said in a scarcely audible voice, "Mr. Ali, your brother needs fifty piasters till the end of the month."

Ali thrust a hand in his pocket and then handed Mahgub the money. Mahgub took it, saying, "Thank you, thank you, dear friend."

He left the library feeling good, asking himself as he tugged at his left eyebrow: When will my pocket be filled with the government's money?

21

He made his preparations. He bathed, ironed his suit, shirt, and fez, shined his shoes, shaved, and combed his hair. He looked like a new person, even if he was still skinny and his complexion sallow.

He arrived rather early at the home of the Society for Blind Women and found it to be a large, elegant house surrounded by a luxuriant and heavily shaded garden. He entered a large hall with a big stage at the end. Rows of green chairs were squeezed together. On either side, balcony doors overlooked the garden. Only a few guests were present when he made his entry. So he calmly selected a seat and started examining the place with jaded eyes. He wondered whether his trip through this house would actually lead him into the government. An unbroken flow of people was arriving. They were greeted by a group of lovely young women. After sitting there for twenty minutes, he found that the number of guests had increased substantially as women and men crowded together wearing the most splendid frocks and magnificent suits. Beauty was everywhere and fragrant perfumes spread throughout the room. Mahgub's field of vision wandered as his protruding eyes hesitated between pretty faces, radiant throats, high backs, and swelling breasts. His blood rushed through his veins with renewed vitality as anxiety shot through his nervous system. He marveled at this dazzling world. Where had it been hiding? The fine clothes and precious jewelry, of which a single piece would suffice to support all the students at the university and all these women—how many there were and how beautiful. It was truly unfortunate that at least one man hovered around each of them. Most were speaking French fluently—these fallen Muslims! It almost seemed that French was the house's official language. How did they communicate with the blind women? Sarcasm (blended with spite) washed over him, but not because he felt chauvinistic about his country's language. He was merely trying to marshal reasons for an instinctive hatred. He wondered where His Excellency, Mrs. Umm Salim's son, might be. He glanced toward the entrance in time to catch the arrival of a dazzlingly beautiful lady, whom he recognized at first sight. He remembered al-Qanatir in a bygone era and recalled the youthful engineer of al-Qanatir and his gorgeous wife. Yes, it was Hamdis Bey's wife, and no one else. Behind her came the bey, followed by Tahiya and Fadil. He trained his eyes on the family as they made their way to their seats in the front row. His pale face reddened as he remembered their trip to the Pyramids. He imagined he heard the car door clanging shut again, leaving him outside. Clenching his teeth, he felt an infernal desire to assault this elegant, haughty maiden. Oh, if only one of these beautiful women would take his arm, allowing him to parade past his "relative's" family! That noble family had taken the trouble to visit this chamber in order to be charitable and merciful. He must prevail, unrestrained by any impediment or law, prick of conscience or moral maxim. When would he sit with them in the front rows? In a magnificent

100

tuxedo, not a journalist's suit! Before leaving this reverie, he spotted in the distance Mr. Salim al-Ikhshidi, who was moving forward with his customary composure and leisurely gait, as if alone in the chamber. He recognized with a nod of his head many of the upper echelon—women and men. Mahgub's eyes followed him till he sat down. Mahgub was filled with admiration and envy. This was a real life, an enjoyable life, a life to satisfy all of a person's drives. Al-Ikhshidi was his role model, and what an ideal role model he was. Then he felt a hand on his shoulder. Turning to his right he saw Mr. Ahmad Badir seated beside him. They shook hands warmly, and Mahgub asked, "Sir, what has brought you here?"

The young man looked at him as if to say: What brings you? He answered with astonishment, "My work! Aren't I a reporter?"

Mahgub told him, "I'm a reporter too—for *The Star* magazine."

They both laughed. Ahmad Badir was about to ask his companion whether he planned to become a professional journalist when the curtain rose. A distinguished lady with a shining forehead and a round, dignified face appeared on the stage. Although almost sixty, she had retained vestiges of her beauty. She was greeted with animated, long-lasting applause, which she received with the serenity of a person accustomed to it. She bowed her head to greet her admirers and then spread out a piece of paper. Mahgub studied her for a long time. He heard Ahmad Badir say in a low voice, "Mrs. Ikram Nayruz, founder of the home."

Right. He had grasped that intuitively. He wondered what role she would play in his life.

Ahmad Badir continued, "She's an old woman but fond of young men!"

Realizing that Ahmad Badir would be chattier than usual, Mahgub actually was delighted, because it was vexing to plunge into a new world without a guide. Meanwhile Mrs. Ikram Nayruz was delivering her introductory remarks in a calm, melodious, and lovely voice. She welcomed her guests, praising the benevolence that had nested in their bosoms. Then she discussed the Society for Blind Women and its lofty goals. She delivered her speech in Arabic, but there was scarcely a sentence that lacked a grammatical error or an ill-chosen word. The two friends exchanged a smile.

Ahmad remarked, "There's no cause for concern. There's no one here who could detect a mistake."

Mahgub pretended to defend her: "Her mistakes can be forgiven. Isn't she speaking a foreign tongue?"

The audience watched a scene from a play by Molière. Madame Thérèse sang a French song that made a profound impression. Next everyone was invited to another room, a circular chamber that had been cleared for dancing. At the back of the room was an Italian band. Tables were set out on either side of the chamber. Music played, dancers danced, and drinks were passed around. The two friends stood chatting at the entrance to one of the balconies as they watched the dancing. Mahgub had never witnessed social dancing before, and it excited his astonished admiration. He saw chests that almost touched breasts and arms that encircled waists. He was amazed that these people could control their impulses. He wished he were dancing. Scrutinizing faces with anxious bulging eyes, he whispered to himself, "Wealth. Wealth equals sovereignty and power. It's everything in the world." His eyes happened upon a swelling bosom that almost made him dream it would poke through the diaphanous white gown. His lust aroused, he raised his eyes to discover his sweetheart's face. What he found was an ugly crone, even if she was a coquette. He nudged his companion, directing his attention to the woman as he whispered, "How can an old woman have such breasts?"

Ahmad Badir examined the woman carefully. He smiled mockingly and then replied, "And how can this charity event take place in a bar?"

Mahgub frowned in anger or mock-anger and replied, "Let the blind women go to hell! A bar's better and longer lasting."

His eyes made the rounds once more and he noticed Tahiya Hamdis. He spotted her dancing with a handsome young man with rippling muscles. He was as tall as Ma'mun Radwan and as powerfully built as Ali Taha. He sensed that he—that other young man—could floor him with a single punch. He scowled and asked Ahmad Badir about him.

His friend said, "A deputy attorney and a nationally ranked tennis player."

Mahgub sighed. Had he been able to become great then—even by a crime for which he would be put to death—he would not have hesitated. What stopped him from being one of these young people? The whole world! The existential forces that shaped history, established social classes, and apportioned fortunes had made Abd al-Da'im Effendi his father and al-Qanatir his place of birth. Then he heard Ahmad Badir whisper urgently to him, "Look at the balcony!" Turning his head that way he saw a lady whose face was almost hidden by a fan of ostrich feathers. Bowing over her hand was a man well advanced in years. When he straightened up, Mahgub recognized him from photos published in the papers from time to time.

Ahmad Badir commented, "This is Anis Bey Ibrahim's wife and the pasha is one of her admirers. She's said to be finagling to have her husband named a pasha."

The music stopped, and many people scampered to the balconies and garden. So the two young men withdrew to the balcony. Ahmad Badir said, "When I first started attending these social affairs, my status brought me endless suffering. I imagined that everyone had nothing to do except to examine me from head to foot. How about you?"

As Mahgub considered his outfit and pale, withered face, blood rushed to his cheeks. Soon, however, he was able to tap into his brashness and insolence. Then he replied calmly, "As we stand here, I feel I'm a man wandering through a herd of cattle!"

He had barely finished his statement when he found himself face to face with Hamdis Bey. His heart pounded violently. He favored his relative with a glance that he wholeheartedly attempted to cleanse of fear and anxiety. He wondered how the man would address him. What would he say? What would he do?

Hamdis Bey recognized him, smiled, and held out his hand, saying, "How are you, Mahgub?"

They shook hands and parted without incident. Astonishment overwhelmed him. Tahiya must have kept the affair to herself! He had never thought that possible. He realized that Ahmad Badir was asking him a second time, "Do you know Hamdis Bey?"

He answered proudly, "Of course, naturally. He's my mother's paternal uncle's son."

"Why haven't you ever told us about this distinguished relative?"

As though still buoyed by his delightful salvation, Mahgub replied in the same tone, "Tuzz!"

They descended the steps to the garden, and his eyes kept searching for Salim al-Ikhshidi. When would he introduce him to the lady? Was there any benefit to be hoped for? He passed clusters of women and men and examined an elite group of celebrities, some of whom were reserved while others were quite vivacious. A strange-looking individual attracted his attention. The gentleman had a huge, ill-proportioned body and a potbelly. He seemed animate matter that had yet to be molded into anything. He walked with his legs splayed apart as though disabled. All the same, he appeared to be esteemed, loved, and honored. He chatted with the high and mighty with an easy familiarity, teasing them and nonchalantly raising his voice while conversing with them or guffawing loudly. Mahgub was amazed and asked, "Since you know everything about everyone, who's that?"

Ahmad Badir laughed and said, "How could you not know him? Azuz Darim was once a respected government official. Then he was forced to resign on a morals charge. So he worked in the private sector. He knew influential people and was returned to government service, prospering there without relinquishing his private enterprise."

"How can he do both?"

"His business is his elegant apartment, which contains a gaming table and superbly endowed young women."

Mahgub thought for a time, feeling depressed and disturbed. How could he excel in such a society? These people surpassed him in his own cynical principles, even without having to reason through them. They were just as irresponsible and daring as he was. So what was the use? Wouldn't it be better for him to become a reformer like Ma'mun Radwan or Ali Taha? His reflections were interrupted by the appearance of a young man as handsome as the full moon. He was slender, extraordinarily good looking, smooth-complexioned, possessed of fascinating eyes, attractive features, and gleaming hair. He moved like a gazelle, exuding charm that was both feminine and masculine at once.

Mahgub could not keep himself from stammering, "My God! How handsome he is! Do you know him?"

Smiling, Ahmad Badir said, "Ahmad Midhat. He's universally celebrated. They quite rightly call him 'The Star of the East.'"

"A government official?"

"Bank of Egypt. He graduated from law school last year. His salary is thirty pounds."

"Thirty pounds! Who is his sponsor?"

Badir laughed. "Idiot, he's his own sponsor."

The bell rang to call the guests, who were scattered throughout the garden, back to the recital hall. They all returned to take their seats in a calm and orderly fashion. The curtain soon rose to reveal a troupe of upper-class maidens in ravishing pharaonic costumes. They danced together a fascinating tableau that was sensitively expressed and that stole everyone's heart. Even Ahmad Badir sang softly a line from Sayyid Darwish's song, "Don't let anyone disparage Egyptian women." The audience applauded enthusiastically and appreciatively for the dancers.

When the beauty pageant was announced next, a tremor of desire and interest traveled through the audience. Onlookers were pervaded by an amazing delight. The panel of judges appeared on the stage. The pageant was the most enjoyable part of the soirée; in fact it was the only segment that aroused universal interest. After scrutinizing the judges carefully, Ahmad Badir smiled ironically and extracted from his pocket a card on which a word or two was written. He folded it till it looked like a twig and slipped it into Mahgub's pocket, saying, "Keep this card till the winner is announced. When you unfold it, you'll find the name of the beauty queen."

Mahgub asked with astonishment, "How do you know?"

"Hush! Pay attention!"

Everyone's eyes were directed to one place as the first contestant was called. She rose on the stage's firmament like a luminous star; she was that brilliant and elegant. She paraded past in a gown of white silk, smiling quietly and graciously, although she failed to disguise her anxiety.

Ahmad Badir remarked regretfully, "In Europe, the contestants are nude! We're satisfied with judging the trappings."

As ironic as ever, Mahgub inquired, "Why don't they choose judges who have inside experience?"

Everyone stared and some held binoculars. Others jotted down their observations in notebooks. The presentation and scrutiny continued without anyone being troubled by weariness or boredom. Faces as beautiful as the moon passed by in succession. Then the panel of judges disappeared for their consultation. A hubbub ensued as debate grew animated and many wagers were placed. The panel soon returned and announced the winner's name: Miss Huda Haydar. Everyone applauded, her father the loudest of all. Mahgub drew the card from his pocket, unfolded it, and found that the winner's name—Huda Haydar—was clearly inscribed on it. With an astonished expression on his face he asked his companion, "What's the meaning of this?"

Ahmad Badir smiled—proud of his prognostication and his behind-the-scenes knowledge. He wanted to leave his friend in the dark, but Mahgub gave him such a hard time he felt compelled to silence him. So he said in a voice that was in no way exultant, "I learned this by accident. I saw the winner at the foot of the Great Pyramid two days ago with the journalists who are on the panel of judges. Does it astonish you?"

Mahgub Abd al-Da'im hated to be truly astonished. So he reined himself in and commented sullenly, "Of course not; nothing astonishes me. The appointment of government officials is rigged, the award of contracts is rigged, and elections themselves are rigged; so why shouldn't the choice of a beauty queen also be rigged?"

❋

The party was almost over when Mahgub remembered why he had come. He saw Mr. Salim al-Ikhshidi heading toward one of the doors. So he said goodbye to his friend and chased after al-Ikhshidi. The gentleman had forgotten all about him. They shook hands and walked together into the next room, which was large and magnificently furnished. Mrs. Nayruz was presiding over a small group of friends. Mahgub summoned his daring to keep from feeling awkward. Together with his patron he approached the distinguished lady. Al-Ikhshidi bent humbly over her hand and introduced him to her in his calm, resolute voice, "Mr. Mahgub Abd al-Da'im, representing *The Star!* A university graduate, he admires the astounding renaissance Your Excellency has orchestrated."

Mahgub bowed to her, and she extended her hand, saying, "I'm proud of the new generation." Then she concluded in French, "The vase is full of dirty water and must be cleansed and refilled."

Mahgub replied in French, "That's true, my lady."

Al-Ikhshidi provided publicity for her in some newspapers, either personally or through the resources of friends. He hoped to add whatever Mahgub might produce to his previous credits. The lady directed some questions to the young man to gauge his cultural acuity, specialization, and aspirations. Mahgub answered suavely. When the conversation veered in a different direction, al-Ikhshidi excused himself and his protégé. As he left the premises, when saying goodbye to Mahgub, he told him, "It's all up to your pen."

Really? Did the realization of his hopes depend on his article about the charity event today? He returned to Giza, lost in thought and under the sway of his dreams. He passed a sleepless night like those back when hunger had kept him awake nights in February. He wandered through a valley of dreams and hopes. Then he recalled at length the soirée where he had spent half of his evening—how lovely luxury was: the spectacular affluence, beauty's manifestations, the splendor of passion, and the insanity of licentiousness. This was the dazzling life for which his spirit pined.

22

he next day, late in the morning, he was pacing back and forth in his tiny room, thinking about this all-important article. What should he say? How should he begin? What would his conclusion be? Then he challenged himself to select the key points. Finally his reasoning led him to an elegant method of displaying these significant points. He spread out a piece of paper, divided it down the center with a line, and gave a title to each section.

The Truth	What I Should Write
1. Ikram Nayruz is the daughter of a man who profited from the British occupation of Egypt.	1. Ikram Nayruz's family has a long, patriotic history.
2. She loves young men.	2. She is a loyal wife and a devoted mother.
3. She is proficient in French but weak in Arabic.	3. At home in Arab and French cultures.

4. The Society for Blind Women is a saloon.	4. Her philanthropic projects.
5. Her guests are just like her.	5. Her guests are just like her.
6. These guests are interested in everything except blind women.	6. Her benevolence.

In this way he educed the key points for this important topic. Then he sat at his desk, preparing to write. He had scarcely picked up his pen, though, when he heard a knock on the door, for the first time since he had moved there from the hostel. Upset and angry, he rose and opened the door. A huge body was blocking the doorway. Then he recognized the man and his heart pounded with terror. It was Salim al-Ikhshidi's messenger—in the flesh. He looked up at the man inquisitively and eagerly. The smiling man told him—albeit in a gruff voice, "His Excellency the Bey wants to see you now."

"Salim Bey?"

"Yes."

"Where?"

"In his office at the ministry." Then the man told him how he had gone as ordered by his boss to the hostel and how the door-man there had described the location of Mahgub's new dwelling. But Mahgub heard none of this. He was dressing quickly and asking himself, "What is it? Is it possible? But so quickly? This is flat-out magic! The woman is an empress. No, a she-devil. Say, instead, a goddess. Oh, how I fear the summons is for something else and that this insane delight will be in vain. But why would he summon me if not for this?"

They set off for the ministry, reaching it around 12:30. He went to the office of al-Ikhshidi, who welcomed him with unprecedented graciousness. He then ordered the messenger to admit no one to the office until he said so. Mahgub sat down near him and the other man turned his calm, triangular face toward Mahgub, but this time the calmness was a mask concealing violent emotions. Smiling, he said, "I've summoned you about an issue relating to your future."

That was what he wanted to hear! His delight would not be stillborn. Emotion got the best of him as he replied in a quavering voice, "I haven't finished the article yet."

"Drop that article and forget about Ikram Nayruz. A much more beneficial opportunity has presented itself like a nearby fruit that needs someone to pluck it."

His staring eyes were full of questions as he replied, swallowing, "With your help, I will."

Al-Ikhshidi took his time, scrutinizing the young man's face with a cunning Mahgub did not notice, because he was observing nothing. Then he volunteered, "I've found a position."

Mahgub's pale faced turned red during the ensuing silence. Then al-Ikhshidi proclaimed, "Level six!"

"Six!"

"A secretary."

Panting, unable to believe his ears, he asked, "Whose secretary?"

Al-Ikhshidi lit a cigarette, showing no mercy toward his fretful companion. Ignoring Mahgub's question, he said, "This beautiful opportunity is a treasure for the person who will seize it but an occasion for regret for anyone who hesitates. Do you remember how the flooding of the Mississippi River some years ago proved a blessing for the cotton crop of our nation, where land was being left fallow?"

The young man was burning with eagerness and declared with firm determination, "It's inconceivable, Your Excellency, that I would hesitate."

Al-Ikhshidi was delighted by Mahgub's eagerness, and his own anxiety was somewhat calmed. Then he continued, "I've previously hinted that to receive you must be ready to give."

What could he give? What did he own that he could give away? He felt choked by this unexpected disappointment, and the gleam in his eyes went out. In a devastated, inquisitive tone he protested, "But . . . how could I give anything?"

"Money's not the only hot commodity on the opportunities market." Mahgub sighed audibly. "Man has some characteristics that are not dependent on wealth. The question boils down to this: Are you daring, cunning, and deserving of good things or are you tossed by your fantasies on life's beach, where they are trod underfoot like dirt?"

His anxiety was visible in his bulging eyes. The young man even removed his fez and wiped his frizzy hair. Then he quickly replaced it and said, "I hope I won't disappoint you."

"That's why I thought of you. My hunch was on the money." He looked at Mahgub with round eyes and asked, "Would you consent to marry?"

He was stunned. It had never occurred to him to get married. He did not say a thing. Al-Ikhshidi was staring at him. In a sarcastic tone, he commented, "Now it's my turn to goad you on."

"Couldn't I have time to reflect?"

Al-Ikhshidi shrugged his shoulders disdainfully and replied, "I thought you were really eager. Why should I wait? There are a thousand and one potential bridegrooms and one must be chosen today."

"Today?"

"In the next hour."

Mahgub sighed. His normal boldness reasserted itself and he said submissively, "Then I accept."

Al-Ikhshidi smiled craftily and said, "That's a good beginning, but there's more."

What did the devil want? There was more to this than met the eye at first glance. The marriage wasn't everything. What more could there be? He heard al-Ikhshidi observe in his odious voice, "But your boldness and decisiveness give me cause for hope. The position is in our office. I held it a few weeks ago. The position is secretary to Qasim Bey Fahmi."

Amazing! Was this credible? Was it truly possible that fate could shower such happiness on him? Why had al-Ikhshidi, whom he had never thought of as chivalrous or generous, chosen him? He was asking him, in exchange for this position, to marry. But what kind of marriage was this? Yes, what was this marriage? Concealing his anxiety, he said delightedly, "Such happiness is like a dream. May God reward you for me."

Smiling and feeling ever more resolute and reassured, al-Ikhshidi said, "Let me tell you about your wife."

This word "wife" produced a tremor in the young man. He gazed at al-Ikhshidi with inquisitive eyes, as if to ask, "Who is she? What does she look like? Why am I marrying her?"

Al-Ikhshidi said, "She's a fine girl from Qasim Bey Fahmi's 'circle.'"

Circle? The young man asked with alarm, "One of his relatives?"

"Almost right; she's one of his acquaintances."

Mahgub swallowed and, pretending not to understand, asked, "A neighbor? He's a friend of her parents?"

Al-Ikhshidi replied simply and scornfully, "Close. His Excellency himself is her friend."

The unvarnished truth was clear. He grasped what was expected of him. He learned the price of this fancy post. Al-Ikhshidi had not sent his office messenger to search for him out of any love for Mahgub's black eyes but to exploit his wretchedness. He definitely loathed al-Ikhshidi, but that was irrelevant. His face was stained a bright red, and he felt his head grow hot. He began to appeal to his effrontery and licentiousness. Yes, why was he embarrassed? What was there to cause him pain? Did he believe

113

in marriage? Did he believe in chastity? Should he feel demeaned by his companion's candor? Here life was proposing to test his philosophy, to ascertain via a real-life experiment whether it was sophistry and intellectual wrangling or a creed to live by. So, inner turmoil, cease. Anger, hush. He should discuss his fallen wife as if speaking about the weather in Brazil. Channeling his contempt and sarcasm, he asked his companion, "A virgin?"

Beaming, al-Ikhshidi replied, "She was!"

They were silent for a time. Mahgub's sallow face was still pink. Then al-Ikhshidi continued, "You certainly shouldn't assume that great men have no faults. The bey is serious about making good on his error. If you support his noble goal, you will earn his approval and prepare a fine future for yourself. A job like this calls for a big heart, vast intellect, and deep cultural background. On the other hand, if you see things through the eyes of the masses, then that will end our relationship. Don't think that I'm running after you. Countless men would accept this offer, although I'd rather have you working with me in the office because I know you're bright and sincere. Moreover, we're former neighbors, and the sixth level is a treasure."

He grasped the ulterior motives that had prompted al-Ikhshidi to send his office messenger to him. Al-Ikhshidi wanted to serve his master and to curry his favor. Perhaps if he did not procure a suitable husband for the girl the bey had seduced, al-Ikhshidi would be obliged to present himself as the ram for the sacrifice. That was clear and understandable. But there were other facts that were even more important to consider. There was the position as secretary and there was the sixth level. Were these worth the sacrifice? Why? Did he care about what people referred to as reputation? Hardly. Did he believe in what people called honor? Damn that. He was quite clear in his own mind about all this. So he had to decide without any hesitation.

Hesitating would mean that he did not live up to his own bold philosophy. Damn him. Could he forget his hungry nights? Could he forget the ful? Could he forget stumbling around the streets of Cairo like a panhandling beggar? Ali Taha was in the library and Ma'mun Radwan was en route to Paris—and he was hesitating? Hamdis Bey could not force himself to sit for five minutes with him and he was hesitating? Tahiya—and at this point he became enraged—had slammed the car door in his face, and he was hesitating? He plucked at his left eyebrow, looked up at his companion, and asked, "Who is she? I want to know everything."

Al-Ikhshidi replied, "You'll learn all that in due time and have no regrets."

Mahgub raised his eyebrows scornfully and said, "So be it. When will the appointment be announced?"

23

Salim al-Ikhshidi sighed with relief and said as he stood up, "Come, let me introduce you to the bey."

Trying his utmost to control his emotions, Mahgub rushed after him. They entered a sumptuous room where the bey was seated at the far end behind a large desk. They approached the desk respectfully till they could almost touch it. For the first time Mahgub saw al-Ikhshidi descend from his high horse and bow submissively over the bey's hand. So he did the same. When he straightened up, he cast a fleeting glance at the seated man, who was in his forties, of medium build, with a handsome face, elegant clothes and accessories, and a pretty little mustache. His appearance suggested that he was a tutor in the school of love. When al-Ikhshidi introduced Mahgub, praising him with deliberate reserve, the bey asked, "Are you a member of this year's graduating class?" When Mahgub answered in the affirmative, the bey told him, "I hope you live up to Mr. al-Ikhshidi's high opinion of you."

Then he held out his hand to indicate that the meeting had concluded. He had intentionally made it an official interview to curb the young man's conceit. Mahgub returned to al-Ikhshidi's room and found him proud and self-satisfied. Mahgub was infuriated with him, but this wrath did not last long, because in spite of everything, he was pleased. He asked politely, "When will the appointment be made?"

"That's the easy part. The memo of your appointment will be drafted today. Then it's a question of preparing the documents that justify the appointment. God willing, all of this will be completed within a few days. Now let us deal with the other matter." He was silent for a few moments. Then he said, "Do me the honor of coming by my home this afternoon."

"Why?" Mahgub asked in astonishment.

The other man replied calmly, "To sign your marriage contract."

Mahgub replied uneasily, "Wouldn't it be better to postpone that till after my appointment?"

"Why?"

Smiling, the young man replied, "So I can deck myself out a little."

"Mr. Mahgub, the best good deed is the most expeditious one. You'll be paid a respectable amount that you can use for your wedding until you receive your first salary payment. The wedding won't set you back anything. Your apartment is waiting for you. All you need to do is to buy some new clothes."

The young man, who had never imagined that everything was already organized this way, was bowled over. The trap was fully baited, just waiting for the mouse, and now the mouse had fallen for it. Would he find honey or poison?

"Won't you give me a week's delay?"

"The marriage contract will be signed today to reassure the hearts of the bride's parents. The wedding ceremony will come after you're appointed."

Mahgub sighed submissively and asked, "Where is the bride-groom's apartment?"

117

"Nagi Street, the Schleicher Building, number 4."

The young man said with astonishment, "That's an expatriate neighborhood, and rents are doubtless high."

"Don't worry about that."

Mahgub asked uneasily, "Why not?"

"You're long on questions and short on patience. Sir, the bey has leased the apartment for a year."

The young man's mind felt muddled. He commented shrewdly, "If the choice were left to me, I would choose an Egyptian neighborhood."

Al-Ikhshidi smiled in a way that showed his contempt for his companion's cunning. He said scornfully, "Expatriate dwellings lack noseyparkers. Thus if the bey decides to visit you, he may do so free of meddlers."

Mahgub glanced at the speaker and found that he was pretending to look at some papers. He felt the blood rush to his head again. His heart pounded violently. He remembered—he was not sure why—his pal Ahmad Badir and Mrs. Ikram Nayruz's party. He imagined himself seated at such an event and his friend the journalist stealthily pointing him out from a distance and talking about him. Always people. People always. Would he allow people to destroy his happiness?

Which would he prefer? To be one of the fortunate few and let Ahmad Badir say whatever he wished or to be one of the wretched masses about whom journalists found nothing to report. He frowned angrily. Was he still hesitating? How could he have forgotten his cherished "tuzz"? What a despicable coward he was. His anger intensified. Then he looked at his companion and said sharply, "So be it."

Al-Ikhshidi replied, "I'll expect you this afternoon."

As Mahgub left the office manager's room, his gaze fell on the facing room, which bore a plaque reading "Private Secretary."

His heart pounded. As he went outside, he began to tell himself: An idiot considers a cuckold's horns disgraceful, whereas I see them as a precious ornament. The two horns cause no harm, whereas hunger . . . . I may be anything, but I'm not a fool. A fool angrily refuses a position on account of something he terms honor. A fool kills himself for the sake of something he refers to as his fatherland. A fool is someone who denies himself a pleasure because of one of the fantastic notions that humanity has contrived. All this is true and beautiful, but I still react emotionally and rebelliously. Why? That's because the intellect is not the only factor guiding our conduct. While the intellect proffers wisdom, the emotions spawn foolishness. So wisdom must eradicate foolishness. Let al-Ikhshidi be my role model. That resourceful fellow obtained his position through treachery and has risen through the ranks because he's a pimp. So forward, ever forward.

Clenching his right fist, he brandished it in the air and quickened his pace as a glimmer of light shone from his protruding eyes.

24

He left his room that afternoon after donning his suit carefully and trying hard to look elegant and nicely turned out. He headed to the road to al-Munira, to al-Ikhshidi's residence. Throughout the day he had been brooding, and his reflections had been punctuated by expressions of wonderment. He would tell himself incredulously: I'm getting married today. The paper on which he had jotted down the main points of his article on the charity event of the Society for Blind Women was still on his desk. How could things have progressed so far? The doors to government service had sprung open, and here he was marching off to pay the price. Marriage? He shouldn't let the word scare him. It was only a word. Frequently what we think of as facts or values are really just words. It was a social custom. In some countries people were polyandrous and in other polygynous. Adultery might be permitted in one country and free love was the law in some societies. There was no absolute law for marriage. So he should deck himself out with his customary courage and daring. He was telling himself such things en route when he remembered his parents and then felt depressed in spite of himself. He was dismayed. His brow dripped with sweat. In his mind's eye he could see his mother, who believed he would never do anything wrong. He could see his rural father, who was eminently good, pious, and jealous. He was getting married without informing them. He did not know when they would hear about it. Was it possible that they would ever learn the truth? Neither his philosophy nor his nerves could help him confront such a challenge. The memory of his parents was a frightening specter that must be expelled from his imagination. How badly he needed to be clear-headed now, as well as quick-witted and self-possessed. Wasn't his bride awaiting him? This fact seemed much more like an imaginary fantasy. Who might his bride be? What would she look like? Who was her family? What were her manners and circumstances? His heart told him she was beautiful; otherwise she would not have attracted someone like Qasim Bey. Likewise, she was doubtless poor. His selection as her bridegroom suggested that, and a rich girl would have no trouble finding a husband. Only the poor are handicapped by honor. What would his conjugal life be like? How would she feel about him? What was the true nature of the tie that would bind them together? How would he receive the bey if he came to visit? What a life! What an experiment! Tomorrow his philosophy and strength would be tested. He would proceed toward his goal, allowing nothing to distract him. His mind could find no solution then for all these problems that the future had tucked away for him. If he confronted them head on, he would know how to overcome them and would emerge victorious as he always had in the past. He felt confident, vain, and conceited. His two feet were striking the pavement resolutely by the time he reached al-Ikhshidi's dwelling. The man opened the door himself. Escorting him to his bedroom, he asked, "Are you ready?"

121

Mahgub, who smiled to reassure himself, replied, "As you can see, bey."

He glanced at al-Ikhshidi and detected nothing to justify his previous veneration for him. Deep inside, he felt a desire to challenge and demean the man.

Al-Ikhshidi said, "The ma'dhun will arrive shortly."

"An Islamic marriage clerk!" Mahgub smiled incredulously.

Al-Ikhshidi, who was smiling too, said, "My friend, you're entering a different world. Now allow me to introduce you to the bride and her parents." With a pounding heart, he followed al-Ikhshidi, an inquisitive look of embarrassment and hesitation in his eyes. He kept appealing to his daring and insolence as his eyes flashed ahead to catch sight of his future. Al-Ikhshidi preceded him into the room, saying, "Here's a new member for your honorable family."

He entered next. His eyes fell on an unexpected face, for he saw Ihsan Shihata, Ihsan Shihata Turki herself, not anyone else. Their eyes turned away.

25

It really was Ihsan Shihata, but not the pure girl Ali Taha had loved so deeply that they had pledged to love and marry each other. Her new story had begun with a single look, which was followed by other things. That had happened when she was returning from school one afternoon, at the corner of Rashad Pasha Street and Giza Street, in front of the mansion known as the "Green Villa." How often she had passed this villa going each way for years! But this day, two handsome and discerning eyes lit on her. They were infatuated with all her comely beauty, and the girl felt the piercing gaze, which left an imprint on her. She saw a distinguished gentleman—if not a pasha surely a bey—of elegant appearance, with a handsome face and a charming, tiny mustache. He looked quite grand and handsome, even though his body was diminutive and he was rather short. Perhaps that fact alone explains why she glanced back after she was several paces beyond him. Then she found he was looking at her. She felt his eyes' penetration and heat with embarrassment. The villa had belonged to an Italian firm's manager, who had sold it to this bey a few months before. It was said at the time that he was an important government official. Some people had jocularly praised him, but she had forgotten all about that. By the time she reached her dilapidated house, she had almost forgotten the bey and his gaze. The afternoon of the following day—also as she returned from school—she saw him in the same place as before. The two comely eyes devoured her as she approached and followed her once she passed. She wondered whether he was there this time by coincidence as on the previous day or whether he had made a point of waiting for her. She walked by without looking back, although she pondered the matter. Halfway down the street, she sensed that an automobile was approaching from behind. She turned her head left and saw a car almost beside her. It was a magnificent vehicle—like a villa on wheels. Gleaming through its windows were the bey's eyes, which directed toward her a curious look that combined a veiled smile, frank admiration, and scandalous impudence. The automobile slowed to her pace. She felt embarrassed and perplexed. She quickened her steps and moved inside on the sidewalk. When she reached the student hostel, the car sped off, turning onto the road to the university and disappearing from sight. Her doubts were discarded. He was flirting with her. Delight and conceit filled her heart. A lightness of spirit and a coquetry she had inherited from her mother overwhelmed her. She sang to herself: The taxi's waiting for me at the door. Then she told herself: This isn't a taxi. It's a limo! Even so, hers was an innocent feeling caused by youthful vanity. The imposing, handsome gentleman, for his part, did not hold his fire. In fact, he carried his flirtation further day by day. So she felt obliged to show him her disapproval and displeasure. Her eyes told him, "This is inappropriate behavior." But he paid no attention to her warning. One day she saw sitting beside him in the automobile a second person with a triangular face and circular eyes. Then the pursuit continued and intensified until the girl grew anxious. She loved Ali Taha and thought it logical that she should end this importunate pursuit. On the other hand, the handsome bey had not made a bad impression on her. To the contrary—her soul rejoiced at his desire and the look of his attractive eyes. She told herself with pain that even though the man was older than Ali he was better looking and more awe-inspiring. She said to herself: If I allowed my heart to speak, I wouldn't know how to discourage it from choosing the mighty owner of the limousine. She began to wonder with rage: Has he repented? When will he get out of my sight? When will he stop dogging my steps? But was she sincere? Or, how sincere was she? She had no candid response to this question. She continued to feel perplexed about what she herself wanted. She began to tell herself almost apologetically that she was pleased he was chasing her. Her feminine conceit and her reaction to his high position in society could have explained that. But one day her father asked her in an insinuating tone, on her return from school, "Haven't you returned to your senses yet?"

Her heart was troubled, and she blushed. Did the man know what was happening on Rashad Pasha Street? Good Lord! Was he still spying on her? She gave him an inquisitive, innocent look. So he said, as her mother joined him, "A man whose status is comparable to a government minister's, although he himself is wealthier and more venerable. Haven't you seen his automobile? Haven't you seen his mansion? What do you want?"

The girl retorted sharply, "What does he want?"

In an unusually gruff voice, which frightened her, Master Shihata Turki replied, "The bey wishes you well. He wishes us well. God wants to raise you to the class of gentlemen and ladies and to proffer sustenance to your starving brothers. His office manager, whom I've known since he was a schoolboy, talked to me. He will marry you. Yes, why not? You're beautiful, and I come from an excellent lineage. God curse these times. How long will you curl your lip? Open your eyes. Your father begs you to help. Your mother implores you. Your brothers cry out for your assistance!" He spoke at length and her mother joined in. That night she did not sleep a wink till dawn. She tossed and turned all night, brooding. The afternoon of the following day, at the usual time, the automobile approached and its door opened. She hesitated a little. Then she climbed in.

How did that happen? Didn't she love Ali Taha? Of course she did. But that hadn't been the type of love that blinds and deafens a person. It was not a love that could withstand fierce trials and violent temptations. She also loved splendor and hated poverty. She groaned under her family's heavy load. The villa was an extraordinary vision. The limousine was a precious treasure. The bey was a god of gold and sovereignty. She had resisted the young law student because it was the first time. Then her parents had kept harping on this and, since that first experience, had left her at risk for any subsequent licentiousness. In fact, they had placed her honor in her own hands. Had it not been for Ali, she would have fallen and ended the debate long before. All the same, privately, she did not want to acknowledge her own weakness. During her sleepless night, she was torn between multiple vows and conflicting emotions. She vacillated between the bey and Ali Taha, between an instant spouse and one in the distant future, between comfort and fatigue, between a life of composure and reassurance and a life of toil and struggle, between an opulent existence for her and her family and one that for the most part would be an endless battle against poverty and ever-present want. Then, with tears in her eyes and a pounding heart, she reached a decision. She convinced herself that she was sacrificing her own happiness for that of the others and that the night that had received her as a tormented maiden would leave her a martyr.

She told herself: I love Ali, but I also love my brothers. It's not right to sacrifice my brothers to my ego. Therefore—and for no other reason—I must yield to my father. I don't love the bey. I don't love splendor. God knows! Thus she climbed into the limousine that had continued to pursue her obstinately and importunately. The automobile was a magic charm and its owner a sorcerer. Ali Taha was both a lover and a critic at once. He loved her but also criticized, instructed, and guided her too, whereas the bey was a charming man of handsome appearance. His words were pleasant and his flirtation insanely entrancing. His eyes might well have been a hypnotist's. When he gazed into her beautiful eyes and spoke to her, she felt mesmerized into sleepy submission. God fully repaid the patience of Master Shihata Turki, because one day a delivery van from the Cicurel Store arrived and emptied its load of fine clothes. Umm Ihsan swayed her head like a torch singer and sang, "Turn aside and come to us." Delight shone in Ihsan's eyes as she studied the silk samples from which she was to choose whatever she liked. Thus began a new page in her history. A few weeks later came an excursion to the Pyramids. The limousine shot away with the distinguished bey and, to his right, a half-moon so beautiful she would have driven anyone crazy. In fact, Ihsan, once decked out and fully accessorized, now that the elegant Cicurel Store and Mme. Grégoire were at her beck and call, became, as the bey put it, "an official insanity." On that day, something was afoot. The automobile broke down and the two passengers got out. The bey said he had a villa nearby and suggested that they should relax there until the vehicle was repaired. They strolled to a beautiful villa surrounded by a luxuriant garden. Then the bey said that since she had graced his country house, he would need to celebrate her auspicious visit. He issued some orders to a servant, and a spread of apples and champagne was set out. He peeled an apple for her and presented her with a glass of champagne, telling her it is a delicious drink and not intoxicating. It was late in the afternoon, and life was at its finest. The window overlooked mellow verdure where the eye could wander endlessly. The sky was blushing with twilight's rouge, and a kite wheeled around overhead, turning away, beating its wings. The cushions of the large chair received her in an affectionate embrace and her feet sank into the thick carpet. The champagne warmed her mind, which then acquired a magical power that transported her from the sensible world to one of spiritual fantasies free of fear, worry, or sorrows. As enchanted fingers tapped on her wrist, tickling her senses and sending thrilling messages through her blood, she heard an amiable whisper more tantalizing than effusive hopes. Hot puffs of breath, repeated like the stabs of a needle, penetrated the area from the pocket of her dress to her cleavage and down between her breasts. She began to resist with listless arms, but eventually despaired and embraced him with them.

❊

Her eyes expressed her alarm, discomfort, and shame. So the bey told her in a calming voice, "Don't think that I have betrayed you. Your future is secure in my hands, with God as my witness."

26

Their eyes met—Mahgub's and Ihsan's—in silent astonishment. Each recognized the other and was overwhelmed by discomfort, feeling distraught. When Mahgub saw her, he almost lost his senses. Ihsan felt stunned when she saw him, because she remembered Ali Taha, the student hostel, and the past that she wished to flee. Glancing around, Mahgub saw Uncle Shihata Turki in a new overcoat and also a plump lady he realized was the man's wife. Al-Ikhshidi perceived the group's bewilderment and said, with a smile, "Perhaps you don't need any introductions."

Uncle Shihata said, "Mahgub Effendi has been our neighbor for the last four years."

This did not come as a surprise to al-Ikhshidi, and that was his reason for making a point of concealing the identity of the two parties from each other before this surprise meeting. He proclaimed, "This is a delightful coincidence. People say, 'Better a devil you know than a stranger.' Shake hands and sit down, Mr. Mahgub."

The young man roused himself from his stupor and approached his new family, greeting them one by one. Ihsan held out her hand but lowered her eyes and pearly face. She had wanted to drape a thick curtain over the past and to escape from it forever. Fate had thrown before her a person intimately linked to that past. It seemed that fate did not feel she had suffered enough. Al-Ikhshidi wished to lighten the tense atmosphere by chatting, but Mahgub ignored him. How could his attention be drawn for a moment from the miracle standing before him? Here was Ihsan Shihata in person! Was this the secret cause of Ali Taha's tragedy? Amazing! How had she strayed? How had the bey managed to seduce her? Ali had trusted her blindly. Was this what had become of Ihsan? Even he, who had never entertained blind trust in anyone, would not have been suspicious enough to predict what had happened. The Ihsan whom Ali Taha had loved no longer existed. That old love was finished. Here was a different, new Ihsan who was holding out to him her hand as their marriage contracted was signed. He had desired Ihsan for so long with such resentful torment. Wasn't the truth stranger than fiction? He realized that al-Ikhshidi was chiding him, "Won't you wake up?"

So he gazed up at him with blank eyes and stammered, "I'm astonished by this coincidence."

Smiling, al-Ikhshidi asked, "How do you like it?"

Without any hesitation Mahgub replied, "No two ways about it—this is a happy coincidence."

Al-Ikhshidi began to discuss the coincidence philosophically, and Umm Ihsan said a word or two. Uncle Shihata thought that he had summed it all up when he said, "The coincidence is God's handiwork and decree. Glory to God." Despite all this, the bridal couple remained sunk in their own reflections, and an apprehensive discomfort dominated the gathering. Then the doorbell rang.

Al-Ikhshidi rose, liberating himself from the tension surrounding him, and exited, saying, "Perhaps it's the marriage clerk."

Their hearts were all pounding. A shaykh entered the room trailed by al-Ikhshidi. He greeted the party and prayed that God would bless his presence there. The shaykh sat down at a table, rolled back his sleeves, and set about his simple but all-important task. His hand, which was covered with thick hair, moved across the paper while Uncle Shihata and al-Ikhshidi looked on. Mahgub frowned a little and tried to force himself to pay attention, setting his reflections aside. Ihsan lowered her dull eyes and looked quite pale. The decisive moment arrived when the marriage clerk turned to Mahgub Abd al-Da'im and instructed him, "Repeat after me: 'Now I accept in marriage Miss Ihsan, daughter of Mr. Shihata Turki, an adult virgin of sound mind . . . ,'" Mahgub repeated this statement with a calm inflection and a clear voice that displayed no emotion even when he pronounced the word "virgin." It sounded odd to him and woke his latent sense of sarcasm and his deep-seated rancor. He remembered what al-Ikhshidi had said when he asked whether the bride was a virgin. The libertine had replied contemptuously, "She was." Yes: was. Why didn't the marriage clerk write, "Who was a virgin"? This constituted fraud in an official document. His marriage was a fraud. His life was a fraud. The whole world was a fraud.

The marriage clerk delivered a sermon that began, "Praise God who made marriage licit and forbade fornication." He carried on with his memorized texts as Mahgub continued his reflections, telling himself: But the bey forbade marriage and legalized fornication! He was endorsing this doctrine by signing a marriage contract that was actually a license for fornication. They were becoming a married couple before God and man. The young man stole a look at his bride and found that her eyes were red and that she was close to tears. He told himself sardonically: A downpour starts with a single drop. Congratulations were exchanged and soft drinks were handed around. It was an unusual wedding; everyone taking part in it felt he was performing a troublesome duty he wished to conclude in the shortest possible time. The bride's parents were relieved but not overjoyed or delighted. The newlyweds sank into their gloomy reflections as anxiety and embarrassment overwhelmed them. At first Ihsan had been amazed when she learned that her hand was sought in marriage. She had asked herself anxiously who would want to marry a bride like her? Then, remembering her respected father, she realized that nothing could be ruled out. Her father had turned a blind eye to her fall. He had handed her to a lover, not to a husband. So why shouldn't there be other people like him? Such a man did exist, and here he was, sitting beside her as her spouse. She certainly did remember him. She remembered how she had rejected his affection back when she could. She despised him but not to excess. She told herself resentfully: Am I not like him or even worse? Each of us has sold himself in exchange for status and money.

Yes, they were married.

27

o the experiment was launched, and his philosophy embraced it with open arms. Mahgub himself, however, felt some anxiety. Although this anguish did not prevent him from taking part and even made him desire it all the more, he never forgot his goal for one moment and worked ceaselessly, as if work provided relief from his whispered doubts. He amassed the documents to justify his appointment. The one that was apparently the most significant was a certificate attesting to his "good behavior and conduct." Al-Ikhshidi and one of his colleagues signed that, causing Mahgub to wonder sarcastically: Who will attest to the bride's character?

He received twenty pounds to set his affairs in order and grasped the banknotes dumbfoundedly, because he had never seen so much money at once. He began to shuffle them carefully, scrutinizing them with awe and disbelief. This was the price of the two horns that crowned his head. Each was worth ten pounds! He found the image of a peasant on one bill and that brought the suggestion of a smile to his lips. He remembered his bedridden father, who was on the verge of starvation, and wondered why the currency did not portray a pasha or the Turkish flag. He told himself ironically that this use of the peasant's picture was comparable to his signature on the marriage contract. With his pocket bulging, he headed to the tailor to purchase cloth for two suits. The man realized that the student was becoming a government employee, since he had only made a single suit for him throughout his four years of higher education. Then, like a proper bridegroom, he went to the Muski, where he purchased two pairs of pajamas, some dress shirts, underwear, socks, shoes, and a new fez. As he packed his clothes into a large valise, his face flushed with delight and vitality. Casting around his small room a malicious look, he remembered those foul February nights and the beanery on Giza Square. To hell with those black days! No matter what it cost him, they would never return. He would have to bring some color to his pallid cheeks, fill out the space between his bones and skin, keep his phenomenal intellect in good form, and slay the dread specter of hunger. To survive, the ostrich stretched its neck as long as a serpent, the lion made its paw as lethal as a grenade, and the chameleon acquired the ability to shift colors. That was what he had done, by different means. Yes, let his aspirations be unlimited and his ambition boundless. He had paid a steep price and the reward must be commensurate. He reflected for a time and then gave himself some advice. Caution? He should do what he wanted but should say only what other people wished to hear. He had grasped this truth from the start. If he volunteered a word or two in praise of virtue, someone would always call him virtuous. Had he candidly declared his enmity to virtue, everyone would have attacked him, egged on by the most sullied among them. Let al-Ikhshidi serve as his role model—al-Ikhshidi who was seen at every charity event. Indeed, he himself might think seriously about joining some of these benevolent societies. Then, remembering his marriage, he wondered again how little Ali Taha seemed to have meant to Ihsan. How had her foot slipped? What might Ali do in the future if he learned that Ihsan had become his wife? He would be aghast; his mind would be torn by anxiety. He would not believe that he—Mahgub—was responsible for his suffering. If he felt obliged to accept this bizarre truth, he would spitefully and rebelliously accuse Mahgub of every meanness, baseness, and reprehensible deceit. So be it. He could accuse him as much as he wished. Let him despise him in every way. Even so, he remembered the loan he had not repaid—fifty piasters. He resolved to repay him that very day. Because of his guilt, he did not feel like seeing him in person and sent the sum by mail. He felt much better then, sensing that he had cut the last thread that linked him to Ali Taha and that it would no longer be possible for him to pay any attention to what the other man imagined or felt or to what he himself had done. He summoned the doorman and gave him the task of selling the contents of his room, promising him a third of the receipts in exchange for keeping an eye out for any letters that might arrive for him. Then he thought of his parents. It may have been the first time he remembered them without annoyance, grumbling, or anger. He fully intended to send his parents two pounds every month, in fact to increase that to three if he could.

The next day he would head to the ministry in the morning. That evening, he would escort his bride to her new nest.

28

He woke up early, went to the ministry, and waited for al-Ikhshidi in his room. The office manager arrived punctually at nine. They shook hands with apparent affection and drank coffee together. While tidying up his desk, al-Ikhshidi commented, "It's incredible! Do you know that most of the requests to waive school fees come from affluent people?"

At that moment at least, Mahgub was not interested in such matters. He felt obliged, however, to pretend to be astonished, saying, "That's really incredible! How do they justify their requests?"

Al-Ikhshidi replied, "There's no pressing need for any justification. All it takes is for one of them to guffaw and tell Qasim Bey, 'The price of cotton has fallen—what else do we need?' So they joke around, exchange pleasantries, and the waiver is granted."

Then, as he always did, he mocked conditions in the country and the stratagems of its senior and junior bureaucrats. Only Qasim Bey was spared his sharp tongue, and perhaps his turn would come in time. Looking toward Mahgub, he said, "Don't forget that your work will require finesse and good management

136

skills." Then, overcome by a proclivity to belittle other people's concerns and positions, he added, "It's actually easy. In fact, it's a game. The truth is that it requires no philosophy or learning— simply finesse."

Mahgub responded attentively, "I hope to profit from your guidance."

"I'm delighted to find a sincere assistant. That's why I reserved this position for you, even though many were competing for it. That's also why we need to work hand in glove, because we have many enemies. Don't let a smile seduce you, because government officials normally humor anyone in power as long as he prospers. Once his star sets, the most generous men simply turn their back on him without sinking in their talons. So let's work hand in glove."

Uncharacteristically, al-Ikhshidi spoke for a long time. Mahgub reflected at length about his plea that they should work hand in glove. He responded mentally: You've encountered someone even worse than you are. Fortune has led you to an assistant cut from the same cloth. His understanding of loyalty is identical to yours. Everything has its special nemesis. My status with the bey is equivalent to yours. If you are his jester or pimp, I'm his lover's spouse.

The burly office messenger entered to announce the arrival of Qasim Bey. So al-Ikhshidi rose and escorted Mahgub to his office, where the bey delightedly shook hands with them and congratulated the young man on assuming the position. He said amiably, "I wish you success and a brilliant future."

Al-Ikhshidi presented him some documents while Mahgub stood there pondering his "brilliant future." They say, "He's a lucky fellow whose boss is his uncle." His new boss was even closer to him than an uncle. He snuck a look at the bey to get a clear picture of the man who had trapped Ihsan and caused her to act rashly. He gazed at him with awe, as if trying to discover his magical secret. Was it good looks, status, or some other concealed quality that Ihsan had found, fortunately or unfortunately, for her? The amazing thing about these men in positions of authority was that they committed major offenses so casually, ignoring what innocents would consider a dilemma or problem, and contriving a facile solution to an affair in the wink of an eye. He himself was just such an easy solution. How had Ihsan fallen? He would feel apprehensive till he learned the truth of the matter. Ali Taha was just as handsome as the bey and younger. So how had she succumbed? Had she married him, he could have said she preferred the bey for his money, but she . . . . Good Lord! Damn these powerful men! They don't take no for an answer. Either Ihsan was a great liar when she promised the idiotic social reformer or she . . . . He had to learn the truth.

The two young men left the bey's office, and al-Ikhshidi conducted him to the "Private Secretary's" office. An elderly office messenger stood by the door. The long room was lined with leather armchairs, and a large desk stood at the end. Al-Ikhshidi said, "I'll leave you in God's care. I'll tell the employees that you are assuming your position today." He himself was wondering whether it would not have been more judicious to employ the young man outside the bey's office. It made him uncomfortable to have in the same office a person with such an intimate connection to the bey. But what could he have done? The situation was precarious, the bey was upset and fearful, and the position was vacant. Had he not stumbled upon Mahgub, perhaps he himself would have become the bridegroom! Time would possibly prove that the young man could be molded to suit his purposes.

He left Mahgub alone in the office. Mahgub was so giddy with delight that he could have danced. He sat on the swivel chair beaming and placed his hand on the telephone receiver.

He had never used a telephone! He began to move to the right and left in the chair. He was obviously an important government official. Tomorrow his belly would be stuffed with meat and vegetables. Down with those philosophers who claimed that happiness consists in simplicity. Wasn't indigestion preferable to starvation's torments?

What mattered were today and tomorrow. To hell with the past!

❀

He spent an hour by himself before his solitude began to seem oppressive. He wanted to do something—no matter what. So he pressed the buzzer. The door opened and the aged office messenger entered. He said politely, "Yes, Your Excellency?" Mahgub blushed. The new rank had a delightful, musical ring to it, although he pretended to be nonchalant. He said tersely, "Coffee." The door had scarcely closed once more when the telephone rang and his heartstrings reverberated in response. He lifted the receiver anxiously and put it to his ear. Then he said in a timid voice, "Yes."

"Qasim Bey's secretary?"

"Yes, sir."

"Is the bey there?"

"Yes, sir."

"Let me speak to him. Tell him it's Muhammad Rashad."

He assumed he had to go to the bey's office to inform him. So he replaced the receiver, cutting the line without meaning to. Entering the bey's office, he said respectfully, "Muhammad Rashad . . . Bey . . . wishes to speak with Your Excellency."

"Send him in."

"He's on the phone."

The astonished bey asked, "Why didn't you transfer the call?"

When he didn't respond, the bey—on seeing the unusual,

bewildered look on his face—laughed and explained, "Transfer the call to me. On occasions like this use the 'connector.'"

He left the room confused, realizing that he had made a mistake. How did he transfer a call? What was this "connector"? Returning to his office, he lifted the receiver and then heard a continuous buzzing. He said, "Your Excellency. . . ."

No one replied no matter how many times he repeated the request. All he heard was a persistent buzzing. He felt even more bewildered and feared that he had committed some new blunder. He felt miffed. He had not realized that telephones have a special drill he would need to learn. He grudgingly summoned the messenger to instruct him in the secrets of telephones. He jotted down notes on a piece of paper so he would not forget what he had to remember in the future. Then his office came to life as a wide assortment of people from different walks of life arrived to request permission to see Qasim Bey Fahmi. He received them calmly, because his natural audacity helped him control his nerves and project a self-possessed, firm façade. He welcomed one of the well-known pashas whom he had only seen from a distance before. The pasha greeted him diffidently, asking permission to see the bey. Although Mahgub presented a calm appearance, he was fighting to suppress his feelings of happiness and joy. He passed the workday in constant motion, unflagging activity, and limitless delight. This nonstop exertion helped him forget his reflections and shadowy suspicions. So without being conscious of it, he calmed down. He left the ministry fit as a fiddle, as if arising from a sound sleep.

He was not the same lad who had rushed to work that morning. He had welcomed beys and pashas, mastered the art of the telephone, and had been called "Mahgub Bey" tens of times. He felt immensely confident and proud. Indeed, his gait and his way of looking at things had changed. He remembered—in the intoxication of this surprising glory—his relative Ahmad Bey Hamdis and hoped he would arrive one day to see Qasim Bey. On entering Mahgub's office deferentially—what a surprise would await him! They would shake hands as equals, and then Hamdis Bey would tell his family what he had seen. So Tahiya would hear and realize that she had slammed the door of her car on a boy who had achieved renown and glory. How he would like Tahiya to see him with his gorgeous wife, who excelled her in charm and beauty. He would like to watch her face as she looked askance at his wife after realizing how fascinatingly beautiful she was.

29

*T*Patience, everything in due time. Life had begun to smile.

hat same day, Mahgub Abd al-Da'im—as previously agreed—went to al-Ikhshidi, who accompanied him to the apartment to hand it over to him. Mahgub carried with him the valise containing his clothes and a few books. Al-Ikhshidi gave him the key to the apartment, saying, "The apartment and all its contents belong to the two of you, except for a small wardrobe in the bedroom."

Realizing that this wardrobe was reserved for Qasim Bey Fahmi, Mahgub blushed and felt a strong desire to kick him as hard as possible.

Al-Ikhshidi observed, "It would be good if you would change the lease to your name."

"Is it currently in Qasim Bey's name?"

Al-Ikhshidi responded coldly, "It's in my name."

Mahgub felt relieved and asked, "How much is the rent?"

"Ten pounds."

Smiling, Mahgub commented, "That's about as much as my salary."

"The bey will pay it. Likewise, he'll pay the cook for you, and other expenses."

They inspected the apartment together. Although it was small, it was beautifully built and elegantly furnished. Mahgub was astonished. He realized that he was seeing many pieces of furniture for the first time. He did not even know what they were called. The apartment consisted of three rooms and a sitting room. To the right of the entrance was a parlor that opened onto a hall leading into a sitting room with a radio. There were two doors on its right-hand wall, one to a bedroom and the other to a dining room. Both of these rooms opened onto a long balcony that overlooked Nagi Street. As he stood there, he quickly recalled his home in al-Qanatir, the student hostel, and his room on the roof of the apartment building on Jarkas Street. Standing there he realized that current realities surpassed in their magic and beauty his prior dreams. Actually the content of dreams is ordinarily drawn from the dreamer's previous sensations and perceptions. He was seeing here luxury articles he had never encountered before. The difference between this house and that in al-Qanatir was as great as between Ihsan and the cigarette butt collector. Both were women, true, but how different. He forgot at that moment what he had always told himself about all women being alike so that Tahiya, Ihsan, and the butt collector were equivalent.

On saying goodbye, al-Ikhshidi told him, "Tomorrow evening you'll find your bride waiting for you."

He departed, followed by the youth's sidelong look.

The next day, late in the afternoon, Mahgub set off for Giza and immediately remembered Ali Taha. Where might he be staying? He knew he was in Giza but did not know where. Had the young man remained true to his promise and retained his interest in the girl? Would his passion tempt him back to her neighborhood and had news of her marriage reached him? Would they run into him while Mahgub was holding her on his arm? He felt anxious, although nothing really fazed him. In fact, he would have liked for Ali to encounter him at that moment and learn everything. He went to Uncle Shihata Turki's home and found the entire family—except for Ihsan—waiting for him. Then he knew for certain that al-Ikhshidi's instructions had preceded him to his noble family. Everyone—Uncle Shihata, his wife, and the six young sons—was sporting new clothes thanks to Qasim Bey's generosity and solicitude. They greeted each other warmly. Uncle Shihata kissed him on the forehead, and he kissed his mother-in-law's hand. He teased the boys and kissed the youngest on both cheeks. As he sat there he glanced at all the faces looking at him and immediately admitted that his bride's house was overflowing with good looks. Her father had handsome features, her mother was beautiful, and her brothers were a matched set of pearls. He told himself that beauty truly is an effective weapon in a poor person's hands. Their conversation flowed nonstop, and the young man shared in it as was appropriate, although he would have liked to leave as soon as possible. Uncle Shihata talked about the hostel and the well-mannered and industrious student Mahgub Abd al-Da'im, who had not been a customer, because he did not smoke and how he—Uncle Shihata—respected students who did not smoke even though (and he laughed at this) he gained nothing from their rectitude. He explained that he was not hosting a party for his daughter's wedding because a good bride is the real festivity and that he had not invited any relatives or family members, who were country folk, in order to spare them the difficulties of the journey. Mahgub assumed that the man was probably lying the way vainglorious people do but, remembering his own parents resentfully, said he had dispatched news of his

144

marriage to his parents and that had his father—a prominent agriculturalist in al-Qanatir—not been ill, he would have come to give his blessing in person. Umm Ihsan spoke about her children, especially Ihsan. Mahgub recognized from his mother-in-law's conversation and tone and from the gestures of her neck, eyebrows, and eyes, that she was a merry, feminine, cunning tease. (He knew nothing of her past on Muhammad Ali Street.) She asked about his position and offered to read his palm. She predicted worthy children and an excellent post in the government.

While Mahgub talked and listened, he kept glancing stealthily at the bedroom door, which was ajar. His eyes asked: How much longer do I have to wait? Finally Ihsan appeared—wearing a diaphanous white wedding gown. Her hair had been braided and then shaped into a turban that highlighted the braids' gleaming blackness, making her complexion look even more luminous. She was accompanied by four women who were said to be her mother's relatives, but he paid no attention to anyone else. Her beauty demanded his attention. He shed his customary scorn as electric sparks shot through his breast and he clenched his teeth. Their eyes met as they greeted each other, and he was filled by the magic that passed via that look. He felt inebriated. Memories of his former suffering and of the tragedies caused by his lust flowed through his mind. Despite all his scorn and daring, he could not believe she had become his—even if through shared tenancy, as you might say. This made him think of his co-tenant, who had been the first. So he felt bad and looked back at her supple body, which the white wedding dress revealed, and felt even worse. Uncle Shihata had prepared for the guests a magnificent dinner, which had cost him dearly. So he invited them to the table. They all rose, preceded by the children's commotion. Umm Ihsan, despite her happiness, was secretly put out, because she would have wished wholeheartedly to celebrate

Ihsan's happy day by making it a day of delight for the entire neighborhood. Al-Ikhshidi, however, had told her bluntly that Mahgub did not have the funds to realize her dream, and she knew her husband had even fewer resources. So she had had to swallow this desire resentfully. Once they had eaten their fill and returned, stuffed, to their seats, there was no longer anything to detain the newlyweds. So they rose to say goodbye to all present. A taxi was summoned and the bride's clothing was carried to it in a large valise.

Mahgub took Ihsan's hand, escorted her through a halfcircle of well-wishers and slowly descended the steps. Umm Ihsan must have run out of patience, because she released a trill that resounded throughout the area and that caused the young man's heart to pound and his eyelids to quiver. The other women received this first ululation like a command for an army to attack and released their own trills that echoed each other, intensifying their staggered explosion, shaking the breasts of all the ladies. The taxi swallowed the bride and groom, who in the musical trills forgot themselves and smiled happily and shyly. They kept looking back at the women standing by the door till the vehicle turned past the hostel onto Rashad Pasha Street.

30

He wanted to speak but did not know what to say. The longer the silence lasted, the more reserved he felt. So he renounced this wish and remained mum. Scrutinizing her carefully, he found that she was looking out the window at the street, turning the back of her head toward him. He was certain that many eyes along the way would envy him this extraordinary beauty who affected him so deeply, and this idea delighted him beyond measure. If only the Hamdis family could see him sitting like this—especially Tahiya Hamdis. Then it occurred to him—after he felt reassured that Tahiya had kept his offense secret—that he should visit his mighty relative one day to introduce his bride, as was customary. This notion tempted his heart so much that it intoxicated him. She still had her head turned toward the street, and so he cast a hungry look at her supple body, passing from neck to shoulder and swelling breasts to slender waist and ending finally with her full thigh. He sighed from the bottom of his chest and observed privately how intense his hunger was and how his blood was boiling. When the taxi stopped in front of the Schleicher Building, he stepped out and then she descended, supported by his hand. They took the elevator and went into the apartment, trailed by the doorman who was carrying her valise. He showed her the way to the bedroom, which she entered, closing the door behind her. He stood there hesitantly and then retreated to a chair in the sitting room and collapsed.

At first he took offense at the closed door, which reminded him of the car door at the Pyramids. He quickly excused it in view of the awkwardness of the situation, although he could not escape his sarcastic nature's bitterness. He told himself: Modesty like this would be more seemly for someone who actually was a virgin. Then, frowning, he wondered what his new life held in store for him: happiness or suffering? He did not hope she would consider him her spouse in the ordinary sense of the word, because he himself could not see her that way. He decided she would privately think of him as a pimp—just as he would secretly consider her a whore. Could a pimp and a whore find happiness together? This was what concerned him—no more and no less. He did not want his conjugal life to acquire any social significance, to produce healthy offspring, or to assume mutual respect. All he wanted was a mutuality of desire, a longing compatible with his, and a lust that mirrored his own. That way he would find satisfaction in a marriage that was a means rather than an end. He wanted love without jealousy as he visited her spring from time to time, without anxiety, thought, or concern, relying first and last on his daring soul, which had smashed all fetters and torn asunder all shackles. As he brooded, his eyes were on the closed door. Should he wait till it opened? If it remained closed, should he stay where he was till morning? He rose, approached the door, and rapped gently. When there was no sound or movement in response, he turned the knob and pushed the door open. He found the room virtually engulfed by darkness, except for a faint light coming from the direction of the balcony. So he realized that she was out there, collecting her thoughts. He went to her, walking softly. He saw her seated to one side, leaning her arm on the railing, looking down at the street. She made no motion in response to his arrival. So he paused, training his eyes on her by the porch lamp's light, and then said, "You were right to come to the balcony. This is one of those hot July nights."

She turned her head toward him and replied, after hesitating, "Yes, it's a hot night."

He was delighted that she had responded and took a chair, sitting near her. When he looked at her, the sight ravished him. Her extraordinarily desirable body set him aflame, and he reflected that he would enjoy this charming body that very night, indeed during the next hour, and felt crazy. This imminent reality intoxicated him as if he were discovering it the first time. No longer able to withstand the ardor of his gaze, she bowed her head. So he stretched out his hand to her chin, lifted her head toward him, and told her in a trembling voice, "Let me gaze at your beautiful face."

Their eyes met for a moment. Filled with fervor, he said, warmly, "Our life has been united by a miracle. Before today, I never appreciated what a significant role chance plays in a person's life. It has every right to mock our logic and all of existence's norms. Perhaps you're feeling forlorn, but you'll survive thanks to your cleverness and education. Just as love can be a prelude to marriage, so marriage can be a prelude to love. A harmonious relationship is the result of souls that coalesce and hopes that unite. Isn't that so?"

Her lips moved as though she had something to say but then froze in confusion. There was the hint of a smile on them. His fervor increased and he said, "You'll discover what I mean and work to accomplish it. Let's strive together to bring it to pass, and then we'll see. . . ."

He told himself: Women can't live without love; you've learned that truth from your reading. She's no doubt in love, but who is the lucky fellow? He assumed that it had once been Ali Taha. He suspected it had been Qasim Bey next. It might simply be a love for wealth rather than for a person. On this reality his happiness depended. He might have been right when he told her, "Perhaps you're feeling forlorn." In fact she did feel forlorn, and he perceived that at first glance. Indeed, he realized that the sensitive and gracious thing would have been for him to spare her that night. He nixed this idea, however, convinced that the raging beast inside him would not accept any postponement or delay. He would be incapable of waiting, no matter what that cost him. Then he put aside his reflections as his natural boldness returned. "Let's go in."

He took her wrist gently and stood up. She rose obediently. Then he put his arm around her waist, and they went inside.

31

When he opened his eyes early the next morning, they fell on the mirror of the fancy armoire. He saw his reflection and that of the precious treasure lying beside him. He leaned on his elbows and then his eyes took a break while he was deluged by memories of the previous night, which had left indelible traces on his soul and body. Ihsan was still sound asleep, and her tresses were spread across the silk pillow. How beautifully pure this skin was! How deep the black of this hair! His breast shook with ecstasy. Then his full lips landed on her smooth cheek.

As he drank thirstily from this abundant well the first week of this new life passed. He quickly realized, from the first moment, that his pleasure—their pleasure—needed to be complemented by something totally novel in order for him to forget what he needed to forget and so she could ignore what it would be best for her to ignore, in order to clear the air for them to enjoy their life in the finest possible manner. He actually experimented with this necessity, about which he had heard a lot. This was booze.

Only a little of it sufficed for both of them, but it had a magical utility. With its assistance, Ihsan dissolved into amiability, exuding magic, and he would rest in her arms, sipping in all the delights of his good fortune. Life on the surface was tipsy with pleasure rendered intoxicating by desire. Beneath the surface, however, there were concealed, turbulent currents. Mahgub could not stop wondering about Ali Taha, Qasim Fahmi, and Ihsan's heart. Occasionally doubt stirred and he would censure his ego and upbraid it, telling himself that it was sheer stupidity that whispered to him, rousing him from his pleasure in order to light thought's fire. He tried repeatedly to shield himself with sarcasm and began to advise himself: Kill doubt. Erase 'honor' from your dictionary. Beware of jealousy. Apply yourself to your passion. Pursue your ambition enthusiastically and remember that you're engaged in the first and final test of your philosophy. Say 'tuzz' now. Say it with your tongue, heart, and will.

Ihsan also had some issues that upset her. She had finally learned her destiny and found her niche. The curtain had descended on the dreams of her earlier life, and her hopes of marrying a mighty bey had been deceived. She found herself the mistress of an amazing residence where two men vied for dominance. She no longer said no. Why should a drowning person fear getting wet? She thought it wise to consider her circumstances. The heart that Ali Taha had awakened had been obliterated and disappeared. The security that Qasim Fahmi had waved before her eyes had not panned out and had vanished. All she was left with was this animal appetite that her father had unleashed early on. Perhaps she pitied Ali Taha, felt resentful toward Qasim Bey, or loathed Mahgub Abd al-Da'im. She did not, however, allow any of these emotions to expand or grow. Her character and circumstances inclined her toward total submission. What could she hope to gain from grieving over a past that would never return? The best thing was for her to direct her attention to the present and future. She should delight in pleasure, accumulate power, spend freely, and shower her family with every boon known to mankind. Only in this way would her sacrifice not have been in vain. Her husband deserved her consideration more than anyone else. She had been ready to despise him more than once, but for what? Because he . . . ? But she had too. . . . She had no more reason to condemn him than he had to condemn her. Actually, something else united them. He was apparently a victim of poverty and ambition like her. Each of them was the victim of a single evil. How appropriate it would be for them to get along and cooperate. Each of them was addressing his issues sagely, attempting as far as possible to banish any suffering. So life continued as pleasurably as drink and a desire to be happy could make it. Mahgub was better than she was at mastering his reservations due to his famous scornfulness. She was a recent convert to amorality. Thus she may well have felt despair while alone. Perhaps she longed for those first, radiant hopes about love and an honorable life. In this regard, she resembled a migrant in a strange land at the moment his new house welcomes him the first night. All the same, she mastered her ailment—and longing is an ailment—with the pragmatism for which women are famous and through a genuine desire for the good things of life. For this reason, when Mahgub asked her one day during the first week while pinching her cheek, "Are you happy?" she immediately replied, "Yes, praise God."

Then the young man told her delightedly, "Life spreads before us. Opportunities are in reach. So let's dash into the flowers and pluck the fruit."

Smiling with pearl-like teeth, she replied, "Let's go and harvest."

He said, "Pay no heed to the crusty maxims by which people define happiness. It's not about life; all of life's circumstances are comparable regarding happiness. It's really a matter of willpower. Happiness will obey anyone who enjoys it by force of volition— willingly or not."

She favored him with a thoughtful look of her extraordinary black eyes. Cautiously and humbly he continued, "If what you desire doesn't exist, then desire what does."

She replied calmly, "There's no need for that." Then, remembering a verse from al-Mutannabi, she recited, "*Any place glory flourishes is fine.*"

He took her hand as if proposing to her, hesitated a moment, and then said in a different tone of voice, "There's one other thing. We shouldn't live a solitary life. Let's take life at large by storm and grab it with both hands."

He wished to enjoy every advantage of his new social status and to sanctify its universally valued if fraudulent manifestations. His need to conceal the deviant aspects of his life was in play here. Therefore, he thought seriously about taking his bride to visit the Hamdis family to heal an old wound and to satisfy his desire to show off. But wasn't there some genuine obstacle to this project?

32

*H*e did not renounce his bold desire, wishing to make this the first step in his conquest of high society. He thought it wise to prepare the way for the visit by telephoning Hamdis Bey. He would be able to tell from the man's response whether the Pyramids story had reached him yet or whether the resourceful girl had continued to keep it from her family. He placed a call to him and received a polite response. So he told Hamdis Bey of his marriage and revealed his desire to introduce his wife to them. The bey greeted the suggestion warmly. Mahgub rushed to tell his wife proudly and joyfully, "I want to introduce you to my important relatives."

On the afternoon of the tenth day of his life in the new apartment they made their preparations for this important visit. Ihsan wore a beautiful dress from her new wardrobe and it highlighted her charming figure. Her magic was completed by the contrast between her jet-black hair, her pure, ivory complexion, and her rosy lips. The young man also shone, now that his health and looks were returning. They took a taxi to Zamalek. Ihsan felt some anxiety and misgivings, but Mahgub smiled as calmly and confidently as if he were heading for his childhood home. They crossed the garden on their way to the parlor, still nourishing these feelings, when they were astonished to see the noble family lined up to receive them at the entrance: Ahmad Bey Hamdis, his wife, Tahiya, and Fadil. Mahgub was delighted by this positive reception. He had been confident it would be a success, if only because women tend to want to scrutinize and criticize other women. They all greeted each other and shook hands. The impact his wife made on the receiving committee was not lost on his bulging eyes. So he felt relieved and rapturous. They sat down and continued to exchange greetings and pleasantries as his anxious eyes glanced everywhere, studying their faces. Without meaning to, he found himself comparing his beautiful wife to Tahiya Hamdis. Tahiya was beautiful, and her beauty had a stamp of elegance and refinement about it, but there was no way that she would be rated as exceptional. His wife was more beautiful than Tahiya. Indeed, she was more beautiful than Umm Tahiya in her prime. Their eyes did not deny or contest this fact. He was ecstatic and told himself with malicious delight: I was vanquished in the tomb on the day of the trip, but today I have my revenge. Wanting them to learn about his wife, he said with his normal termerity, as he pointed toward his girl, "Ihsan is the daughter of Shihata Bey Turki, a major tobacconist. Don't you know him, Your Excellency?"

Ihsan blushed and looked down to hide her discomfort. For his part, Ahmad Bey Hamdis wrinkled his eyebrows as he searched his memory. Then he said apologetically, "Unfortunately I can't place him." Turning toward Ihsan, he added, "It's our great honor!"

Gesturing toward his wife once more, the young man laughed and said, "She's a former classmate; I met her at the university."

The bey and his wife smiled, and Ihsan smiled as well. She was appalled by Mahgub's recklessness, not knowing how far he would go. Fadil was looking languidly at the bride, but Tahiya could not take her piercing eyes off her. She had grasped the true motives tempting the young man to make this visit. So she felt even more contempt for him and her glances at the bride were clearly scornful and mocking. Hamdis Bey's wife began to discuss the university's women students, saying, "The university is a place to prepare for a career; that's why Tahiya has chosen a different path." She asked the bride, "Weren't you planning to look for a job when you enrolled at the university?"

Ihsan, who was annoyed by this conversation and concerned about the consequences of lying, felt, nonetheless, that she must reply. "Of course, Ma'am, but everything is a matter of fate and destiny, as they say."

Tahiya wickedly asked her, "Don't you regret this change of plans?"

They all smiled, and Mahgub laughed, as though her taunt pleased him. He said, "God forgive me. Ihsan was a brilliant student. She frequently amazed M. Lechot, the philosophy professor, with her intelligence. He long opposed her departure from the program."

He looked at Tahiya to check her eyes for the impact of his words. He found that she was gazing at him contemptuously and ironically. He did not feel angry. In fact, he was secretly delighted. Then a Nubian servant entered with refreshments. They drank with relish and silence prevailed, as if this were an intermission.

Hamdis Bey's wife picked up the conversation again, dredging up old memories as she recalled the small boy who now made an appearance as a worthy husband and the head of a new household. She spoke of time, of its remarkable rapidity. Then she asked the young man, "How are your parents?"

"Praise God," Mahgub answered quickly. Then he immediately felt depressed. The lady asked him, "Didn't they attend your wedding?"

"They were prevented by my father's ill health."

After offering a prayer for the man's full recovery, the lady asked, "How is al-Qanatir?"

"As beautiful as when you lived there."

"It's amazing; we haven't been back since we moved."

Smiling, Ahmad Bey Hamdis asked, "Are you spending your honeymoon in Cairo?"

Mahgub was delighted by this question because it opened new areas for conversation. He answered, "My position as secretary to Qasim Bey Fahmi doesn't allow me any free time at present."

At this point—to explain why they were in Cairo in July, in case there was any doubt in his mind—Tahiya said, "My father usually takes his vacation in August. Then we'll all travel to Europe." Changing her tone, she asked him with special emphasis, "Haven't you taken Miss Ihsan to see the university's excavations?"

His heart felt troubled, and he ran his eyes round the faces of those present. Finding that everyone was smiling and that there was no indication in their expressions of any suspicions, he sighed with relief. Controlling his emotions, he replied, "No." Then he added spitefully, "We'll no doubt go there soon, once we buy a car."

Just as spitefully, she said, "The nicest trips are those on foot."

Hamdis Bey asked about Qasim Bey Fahmi, who—he said—had been his comrade when they studied overseas. He promised to commend Mahgub to him. This link, which was unforeseen, troubled him. What would happen if Hamdis Bey discovered the secret behind his marriage? He felt an icy hand clutch his heart. Since this visit was merely a chance to get acquainted, he did not wish to prolong it. So he rose and they asked leave of their hosts.

On the way back, Ihsan snorted, "I take refuge in God from you!"

He guffawed and said sarcastically, "Be daring. Lying is as much a form of speech as telling the truth; but it's more beneficial."

"What if we're found out?"

He replied with exasperation, "What if, what if—always what if. This phrase 'what if' is a recipe for failure. When inserted into a sentence, it negates the sentence's usefulness and frustrates the protagonist's intent. Don't say, 'what if.'"

Ihsan laughed and replied, "Your distinguished relative's wife is a nice lady."

Stealing a crafty look at her, he asked naughtily, "What about Tahiya? What a fine girl she is!"

Ihsan remained silent, not knowing what to say. Finally she stammered, "Right."

He was watching her mischievously and felt supremely delighted. He returned to the apartment like a triumphal victor. The rest of the evening he felt grand, until the telephone rang. When he placed the receiver to his ear, he frowned and his enthusiasm for life waned, as if cold water had been thrown on his flaming heart, which had been dancing merrily. The speaker was Salim al-Ikhshidi, who informed him that the bey would be visiting the apartment the following evening.

33

*H*e began to recite, *"No wound hurts a dead man"* the next day as evening approached and he was preparing to depart. Then he asked himself when his feeling of being wounded would die? He was supremely confident in himself and his philosophy, but his consternation made him feel that his philosophy—when it emerged from his brain to the world of realities—might encounter the same difficulties a projectile does on emerging from a cannon, when it explodes and disintegrates into fragments. He attempted to recover his normal sangfroid and coolheadedness. He tried to say "tuzz" but failed, or—as he put it—failed temporarily. He began to wonder whether she knew. Looking at the telephone, he conjectured that the bey had dispatched the happy news to her. The telephone was the apartment's second pimp. What might her true feelings be? Was she delighted by this all-too predictable tryst? Was she waiting for him eagerly or lackadaisically? Should this pretty head be split open as if it were a coconut to see what was inside? As the serpent of jealousy poisoned his heart, releasing its lethal venom, he left home and walked along Nagi Street without any destination in mind. The most he wanted was to regain his self-control or to return to his senses.

He found himself in front of a bar called "La Rose." So he made for it without any hesitation, as though this had been his goal all along. People seeking beer were flocking there, fleeing from July's scorching heat and thronging the sidewalk tables. Mahgub hated crowds and sought a place inside. The sole person near him was a young man who was alone with his drink. Within five minutes of his arrival Mahgub was raising a glass to his full lips and draining it. Then he clapped his hands to order another. He drank with uncharacteristic fervor, even though this was the first time in his life that he had set foot in a bar. His mind continued to reflect busily, not swayed by his surroundings. His anger at his anxiety was no less severe than his anxiety itself. It was intolerable that he should feel upset about a trifling value like those he had rebelliously rejected. Was it really his honor that was troubling him? What was honor? Hadn't he freed himself from all those shackles? Of course he wasn't angry about an affront to his honor. Honor wasn't something a person should get agitated about. He was suffering from jealousy. He thought for a time and then asked himself: Is jealousy something natural or is it a social construct like honor? No, it's definitely part of human nature. Animals suffer its burden just like men. We are jealous while in love as long as we think ourselves fit to be loved. That was what he told himself, without feeling fully convinced or relieved. Something still troubled him. Might not this jealousy threaten to destroy everything he had gained via his philosophy and liberation? He criticized, analyzed, and dissected, but all the same frightening images presented themselves. An automobile came to a stop in front of the Schleicher Building. The elegant bey got out, took the elevator, rang the doorbell. The door of the apartment opened.

161

"Good evening, bride. Your real groom has arrived." How would she receive him? In the same room on the same bed? He clapped his hands violently to order another drink.

Then he happened to notice the young man alone with his drink—his drinks. He realized that the man was staring at him with astonished delight. The young man had been observing him since he arrived and had noticed his agitation and involuntary gestures, wondering what was upsetting him. The delight and pleasure, however, were attributable to his advanced state of inebriation. When their eyes met, the man smiled. So Mahgub smiled back. Drunks make friends quickly, even if their affection is superficial. They exchanged greetings, and the stranger appeared to be appealing to his new friend for comfort in his loneliness, which inebriation had rendered unbearable. Mahgub sought refuge with him from his thoughts and sorrows and invited him to his table. In no time at all they were seated facing each other— two tipsy young men who attached no importance to anything. They introduced themselves. Then the young stranger said, "I saw you engage in a fierce debate with yourself and felt like intervening to comfort you."

Mahgub laughed so loudly it was clear that sobriety had fled. He asked, "Was I really talking out loud?"

"Yes, you were furious . . . even spiteful."

He was forced to speak because he had been invited to converse and because he felt like getting some things off his chest. He saw no harm in this, for his condition and his friend's allowed for rash and impudent talk that was uncensored. He asked, "When does a man talk to himself?"

"On rare occasions."

"Give me some examples."

"In the flush of delight, during extraordinary grief, or in other conditions unrelated to either of these."

"What does that leave?"

"Occasions when a man debates with another person."

Clutching his glass, Mahgub observed anxiously, "I can hardly tell heads from tails."

"Me too! In a social congress, as in a political one, it does not matter whether you understand what is said. The important thing is to say something."

"Anything at all?"

"Whatever you feel like."

This suggestion pleased him. So he cast thought aside and—his protruding eyes red from drink—began, "I'm in this room while the ram's in the field."

"Muhammad wrote down the lesson."

"Work in your world as though you would die tomorrow and prepare for the next world as though you would live forever."

"But you won't live forever; you may not make it to tomorrow morning 'cause you're drinking too much."

"Then let's order another round."

"What does the fact that bars are full of patrons suggest?"

"That the 1923 Constitution was better than the 1930 one."

"Do you think the 1923 Constitution will return?"

"Where is it now?"

"In Saad Zaghlul's tomb with the pharaohs' corpses."

"They should keep it there till we deserve it."

"Are you a member of the Wafd Party?"

"No, I'm a Hanbali."

"What's the difference between the two?"

"A Hanbali becomes ritually impure just by thinking of a dog."

"How about the Wafdist?"

"He becomes ritually impure just by thinking of patronage."

"Then you're a liberal constitutionalist!"

"Me? I'm in the field."

"Then you're a ram with two horns!"

Mahgub was stunned and upset as if he had been roused from his stupor by a hammer. He shot a fiery look at his friend but found he was smiling light-heartedly, preparing to respond to anything Mahgub flung at him. Forcing himself to be positive, he asked the young stranger, "Tell me: Does a pimp have a good life?"

The young man laughed along with him, seeing that Mahgub was throwing more wood on the fire. Wishing to be of assistance, he replied, "You should know!"

Mahgub laughed so loud the room shook. Then he said, "Tell me what you know about the different forms of infidelity."

"There's blind infidelity when the victim is in the dark—like my lover's husband."

"That's one."

"Then there's a type when the husband knows about the infidelity but pretends he doesn't—to avoid causing trouble. This variety is widespread in some circles."

"Two."

"Infidelity the husband chooses either for his own pleasure or for some other boon. Are you married?"

He laughed again and continued laughing to mask his nervous tension. Then he said with disguised resentment, "There's a fourth type that combines the characteristics of the other three. This is how it happens to you. First of all you don't realize you have a problem. Then you catch on but pretend not to know, to avoid a fight. Finally you adjust and learn to enjoy it."

They burst out laughing again. Then the young stranger said in a mock-serious manner, "The fact is that infidelity is one of the knottiest problems for marriage in modern times."

"The truth is that marriage is one of the knottiest problems for infidelity."

"You're right. Otherwise, why do you suppose young people are avoiding marriage? They continue to live at home instead."

"Living with relatives is more fun when you don't have to pay."

They spoke deliriously for a long time, without feeling bored or tired, until almost midnight.

❋

He felt like roaming the streets before returning home. He chanted as though moaning, "I'm in the room and the ram's in the field." Then he began to say, "I'm in the bar and the bey's in the room." But he was at the apogee of intoxication and delight, and his rapture had reached such heights that all his sorrows had melted away. It seemed to him that nothing in the world equaled an atom of despair. He found the power that would enable him to implement his philosophy should he so choose, without any hesitation, reflection, or emotion. He realized then that his philosophy and liquor were essentially identical. Returning home, he entered the bedroom, where everything was calm and still. She was sound asleep. He stood at the center of the room, staring at her face with dull, red eyes and remained there until it seemed the earth was starting to revolve. He thought of something that cheered him, although he did not pause to think it through. Instead he implemented the idea in less time than it had taken him to think it up. He went over to the bed and threw himself on top of her as though preparing to do Swedish calisthenics. Ihsan awoke. A scream sprang from her mouth. She stared at him with terrified eyes. Then she pushed him off after realizing what was afoot. She shoved him away furiously and resentfully and yelled at him, "You're drunk! You almost killed me! Get away!"

He began to stare at her in bewilderment, filling his eyes with her indignant, angry face. Then he smiled. His smirk was either meaningless or a smile of delight at the pain and rage he had caused her. She became even more resentful and said sharply, "You've broken my ribs with your insanity. Get away from me. You're drunk. Don't sleep in this room."

The smile stayed plastered on his lips. Then a light laugh escaped from his mouth. When her anger intensified, he lapsed into laughter so profound it shook his very being.

34

The next morning he awoke late and rose with a headache, feeling tired. He had slept on the chaise longue. He looked at the bed with fearful eyes but found it empty. He remembered the previous night, and the memory horrified him. Then he shrugged his shoulders dismissively and left the room. He found her in the sitting room. She looked at him with a frowning face and he felt uneasy for a time. With eyes downcast he smiled and asked her in a gentle voice, "Not still angry?"

She replied sharply, "When you're drunk you turn into a crazy beast. Don't ever get drunk again. Drink a glass or two the way we do: that's okay. But for you to return after midnight staggering drunk and acting in this disgraceful way: that's not acceptable."

They moved to the dining room, where they ate breakfast, silently at first. Then they exchanged a few words, and left the room on good terms. He went to the ministry shortly before noon to find that the bey had journeyed to Alexandria to spend a few days in Bulkeley. He sat in his office glancing at the newspapers.

A short time later he received an unexpected visitor. The door opened and he looked up from the paper to see Ma'mun Radwan heading toward him. A look of astonishment appeared on his face and then he rose gaily. The two friends shook hands warmly. Ma'mun took a seat and said, "Congratulations. Congratulations."

Mahgub realized that he was congratulating him on the position. That delighted him immensely and he replied, "Thank you. I thought you were in Tanta."

"I returned two days ago for personal reasons, and the night I got back I ran into Mr. Ahmad Badir at the university club. He told me about your appointment, and I was tremendously delighted by that."

Ahmad Badir—he felt rattled by the mention of that significant name. He wondered what this journalist, who knew all of society's scandals, might have learned. What had he told Ma'mun Radwan? He looked carefully at his friend but found his expression as calm and pure as ever. His appearance suggested a clear conscience untroubled by bad news. Pretending to smile, Mahgub asked, "How is he? I haven't seen him for quite some time. He hasn't come to congratulate me."

Ma'mun smiled and replied, "Some things have escaped your notice. News of your appointment was published in his newspaper. As he explains, he thinks you ought to thank him."

They discussed Ma'mun's overseas study, administrative and technical positions in the government, and the career of teaching at the university and in the secondary schools. Ma'mun criticized the prevailing system that did not allow specialists to hold posts in their field, and Mahgub was uncomfortable about a lack of respect for administrative positions. He told his friend that these had a special glory that teaching positions could never claim. Ma'mun understood glory in quite a different way. All the same, they presented their views in a comfortable, tolerant fashion.

Their conversation raised some personal concerns, and Ma'mun confessed he had come to Cairo for reasons related to his marriage. Then Mahgub informed him that he had married. The young man congratulated him once more and prayed for his success. Then he said, "I met our friend Ali Taha yesterday and spent a long time with him."

Mahgub's heart pounded at this sudden change of topic and he felt anxious. Had Ali Taha's name come up by chance or did Ali know about his marriage and tell Ma'mun? It was not possible for his marriage to remain secret, and Ali Taha would definitely learn about it some day. But how had the news gotten to him? How did he understand it? He looked at Ma'mun, and their eyes met. He detected discomfort and suspicion in those pure black eyes. So he felt no more doubt. Ma'mun's eyes were a clear mirror, innocent of any cunning or deceit. They were obviously asking him, "Is it really true what he said? Have you really betrayed your friend?"

Finding it pointless to force his friend to ask first, he said, "How is he?"

Ma'mun replied gravely, "Fine."

They were silent for a moment. Mahgub bowed his head. His conjecture had definitely been confirmed, but how much of the truth was known? Those who knew the whole truth—Ihasan's family, the bey, and al-Ikhshidi—would not be able to disclose it to anyone, because that disclosure would harm them. If Ma'mun knew the truth he would never have visited him. It was not like him to pretend to show respect for someone he thought deserved his contempt. He had merely come to hear Mahgub's defense against their friend's accusation, which was quite simply a charge of betrayal, not an accusation of marrying a certain kind of girl because he wanted a job. This was plainly the truth of the matter. Feeling satisfied with his reasoning, since he wasn't

169

concerned about Ali's grief or about what Ma'mun thought of him, he looked at his visitor with his customary audacity and asked, "What's troubling him?"

Ma'mun did not know what to say. Feeling uneasy, he bit his lip and remained silent. Mahgub laughed listlessly, and then said as if answering himself, "My marriage."

Ma'mun asked eagerly, "Really?"

Mahgub responded tersely, "Actually, I married our former neighbor Ihsan Shihata Turki."

The other man's face revealed his astonishment and discomfort. Smiling, Mahgub said, "But I didn't do anything wrong."

He explained how the relationship between Ali and Ihsan had faltered and finally been terminated. He confirmed that he had not stepped forward to request her hand until afterward.

With the candor for which he was known, Ma'mun asked, "Aren't you responsible for the relationship's problems and termination?"

Mahgub said with great certainty, "Absolutely not."

The visit concluded after that. As he shook hands with Ma'mun, Mahgub felt that the young man was saying a last farewell to him. When he heard the door slam shut, he spat contemptuously and angrily and muttered with intense resentment, "Tuzz!"

35

After lunch he stretched out in bed, but his eyes were still open. She was sleeping beside him as usual, and he began to listen to her now familiar, regular breathing. Then he yielded to the turbulent current of his thoughts, which had denied him the pleasure of sleep. Today Ma'mun had parted company with him. Not that long before he had parted company with Ali Taha. Thus his ties to the people closest to him had been severed.

Friendship had never been anything he craved, but he felt alienated and solitary, as if he were in one valley and the rest of the world in another. Yes, he had never taken any pains to befriend anyone, but more than one person had befriended him, leaving him the feeling of being on amiable terms with people. Now that the slender threads tying him to other people had snapped, one after the other, he was falling into a deep isolation. Before, the oddity of his ideas had occasionally afflicted him with a sense of desolation. As he put some of his ideas into practice, this feeling of desolation increased, and he felt that he was alone in a valley while the rest of the world was in another. He asked himself apprehensively how he could expel these clouds from his breast. There was not a single individual he liked in his world. With the other government employees he knew there was merely an obligatory form of camaraderie. Salim al-Ikhshidi's only concern was his personal self-interest. Where would he find the antidote? He glanced at the face of the person sleeping beside him, and heard her regular breathing. Yes, she was his consolation, his solace, the essence of what remained to him of his life. If he could win her, he would complain of nothing. His anxiety today was not really inspired by his rupture with Ma'mun so much as by remembering Ali Taha and his passion. His heart fell prey to jealousy, and he no longer believed that marriage was merely the safety release valve on the boiler, as he had liked to say when asked about love or women. His perceived need for a wife was violent and powerful. Perhaps this was a consequence of his feeling of desolation or perhaps he was responsible for it. Even in his current condition he didn't believe in love the way Ali Taha understood it. He didn't force his eyes to look to the heavens; there was no dream of ideals and fantasies, even though he experienced his need for the girl as a tyrannical, brute force that wasn't merely a result of his sexual maturation. It was a reciprocal desire and a reciprocated longing, without which he would not feel he had shaken off his desolation and achieved any solace. This tyrannical, brute force mocked domineering intellects, presumptuous souls, and sarcastic philosophies. He smiled ironically and started to say, "To hell with all this despicable jealousy." What point was there to the vanities of this life if the world lost its savor in response to nothing more than a dismissive gesture from this gracious animal? The reality of his new feelings wasn't lost on him. Initially he had agreed to the marriage as part of a self-interested bargain and had hoped to overcome his irregular status by

172

embracing absolute freedom and limitless ambition. Now, however, he craved more than his wife's body. He craved her love. If his fortune had united him with a different woman—not Ihsan, the girl he had adored in the old days—perhaps the situation would have been different. With Ihsan, however, he had no choice but to love her when his mind was tormented by such thoughts, which he considered a warning that threatened his existence and life. He told himself sadly: Perhaps they're symptoms of a passing malady caused by my frightful desolation.

※

That afternoon they were sitting together on the balcony, drinking coffee. He had been unable to extricate himself from his ruminations for a moment and looked tired and anxious. His bulging eyes kept glancing at her face until she noticed. Sensing his fatigue and anxiety as well, she guessed that the cause could be traced back to the previous night. She said nothing but cast him an inquisitive glance. Wanting to explain how he felt to her, he said, "I didn't sleep after lunch."

Pretending to be indifferent, she asked, "Why?"

He did not answer her question, because he felt some force prompting him to plunge into the enigma that overwhelmed and upset him. Resting his eyes on her, he said, "You're a secret I need to understand."

Her beautiful face, which still looked drowsy, revealed her astonishment. She stammered, "Secret?"

"Yes. I think we ought to be candid with each other."

"Be candid?"

He ignored her astonishment, thinking it a charade. He explained, "Your life poses troubling questions for my soul."

She closed her eyes, made no response, and looked glum. But no force, no matter how powerful, was going to dissuade him from proceeding. He said, "Candor in our situation is priceless. Each of us must understand the other so we can cooperate to perfect the happiness of our life together. Never forget that we're partners and that anything outside of this partnership is ephemeral."

Draining her coffee cup, she put it back on the table between them without uttering a word or displaying any desire to speak. So he continued, asking her boldly, "Why did you do what you did?"

She turned red and retorted sharply, "Why did you agree?"

He responded quickly in a tender voice that sounded apologetic, "I'm not trying to get even; I simply wish to understand. Why? Didn't you . . . ."

He closed his mouth involuntarily. He was blushing. Then he resumed, "Ali Taha?"

She attacked him immediately in a sharp, angry tone. "There's no need to mention him."

So he asked in a weak voice, "And Qasim Bey?"

She frowned and began to chew passionately on her fingernail. Then she said sharply, "My reason for making his acquaintance was identical to yours for agreeing to this marriage."

Feeling relieved by this answer, he said tenderly, "Don't get angry. As I told you, I'm not trying to settle accounts. I would simply like to know: Don't. . . . I mean, your heart, yes, your heart!"

"My heart! Candor will achieve nothing—or nothing good. My heart? What are you asking? Aren't we . . . happy?"

"Yes, of course."

He said this quickly. After some reflection, he asked her with amazing boldness, "What if I forbade you from seeing the bey?"

Huffing disapprovingly, she said, "I would obey my husband."

He sensed the sarcasm of her remark, and that wounded him deeply. He wondered if he had gained anything from his daring interrogation, for he found himself feeling the same anxiety and apprehension he had before. He realized that Ali Taha was still responsible for his anger and resentment. "There's no need to mention him." What did that mean? She had said it angrily.

He was angry that he felt so weak. Why shouldn't he combat these malignant emotions till he destroyed them? Should he succumb the way other idiotic human beings did? Let her love Ali Taha or Qasim Bey. Let the bey visit every night if he wanted. He should respond to all of these provocations with superhuman scorn and mockery. That was his challenge—no more, no less. At the same time, his ambition should know no limits. Every malady has its antidote, and the antidote for the desolation affecting him was glory and liquor. Since he himself was a victim of exploitation, he had to exploit others. On the morrow, he would search for houses of ill repute and love women of all kinds. If his wife's secret ever was discovered, people would say, "Her husband corrupted her with his wantonness. He's nothing but a debauched young fellow." He sighed with something approaching relief at this conclusion to his deliberations. The relief was short-lived, however, because he remembered, sullenly, that he was always afraid of people, that he feared them more than he should, and that this fear stood in stark contrast to his philosophy. Why should he stumble and feel anxious? When would he raise his life to the level of perfection he desired?

36

e did not attempt a conversation like this again and did his utmost to avoid anything that could rile their composure or trouble their peace of mind. To defend his happiness, he fought with a desperate brutality that spared nothing. If true married life was not an option for him, he played it to perfection—like an actor who adopts his role so fully that he forgets himself and really laughs and weeps. They presented themselves to the world as a happy couple. Both of them wished to succeed and yearned for happiness. Whenever they felt any estrangement or coolness, a shared drink (or two) would fix anything that threatened to cause tension. He was determined to devote all his time to his new life so that insinuating whispers would find no path to his heart. Since his job consumed most of his day, he thought he would plunge into the socializing he had begun with his visit to the Hamdis family. He would fill his leftover time and reap any pleasures of a social life's external manifestations that would be showered on a person like him. He discussed the idea with Ihsan, seizing a favorable moment one day to tell her, "I've gotten to know a select group of young government officials and some other distinguished individuals, and one of them has invited me—invited both of us—to a party he's giving for his son's birthday. So I joyfully accepted."

She looked up at him with large, black eyes, not knowing what to say. He continued enthusiastically, "We shouldn't sit home. Look at al-Ikhshidi. He knows all the top figures in high society, and those ties support his life and serve as a foundation for his future."

Deep inside, she hankered for diversion, consolation, and fun. She wanted to see and learn and forget. So she embraced the suggestion. After her smile had already signaled her acceptance, she said, "Let's go."

The young man was delighted. He had always wanted her to share his interests and hopes. He felt instinctively that if he succeeded in drawing her into his ambitions, he would be guaranteed a huge success. So he was pleased and said, "A person plunging into this extraordinary life is like a daring explorer who can't return empty-handed. Because of my job I enjoy an excellent status and you hold a lofty position because of your beauty."

They attended the birthday party. Ihsan made a noticeable impression with her fascinating beauty, and Mahgub relied on his audacity to help him play his role. He was able to create a fitting opportunity to reveal his close relationship to Ahmad Bey Hamdis. For her part, Ihsan won the admiration of a young swell named Ali Iffat, who invited them to share his "Baignoire" box at the Fantasio Theatre two days later.

The remaining days of July passed with a vibrant, merry social life. They frequented the cinema and summer receptions. He was invited to cafés like al-Bodega, Groppi's, and the Soult Parlour. One day he confided his delight to al-Ikhshidi, who grimaced contemptuously and said, "The upper crust are out of the country right now. Cairo's real life will return by the middle of October."

177

This idea appalled him, but he was content with his new acquaintances. Perhaps such people were closer to him than the elite who were touring foreign realms. One thing did upset him, however: the expense of this jolly, entertaining life, which obliged him to pay precisely as great attention to his clothing as women did and to purchase expensive brands and select beautiful colors, taking every precaution that a critical eye would not find him in any outfit more than once. Among these young men he had befriended, he found no one who discussed the Arab identity or debated socialism or Auguste Comte's ideas. Many were university graduates, but they came from provincial schools and had not a word to say about the Orman Gardens or the student hostel in Giza. He found that he was growing fond of smoking and of watching the gaming tables.

But how could he compete in this life with his tiny salary? Yes, Qasim Bey paid all the bills for his apartment and his spouse, but that left all his own expenses, which grew day after day and became more diversified by the hour. After reflecting about this for a long time, he told himself: People like me rise quickly in government; I can't fall behind!

※

Society life agreed with Ihsan. She was attracted by its diversions and merriment as well as by the opportunities it afforded to show off, boast, and elicit admiration. She was interested in novelties, and a spirit of curiosity and enthusiasm became an established feature of her existence, saving her from having to brood about her life—past, present, and future—and from surrendering to reflection.

She delighted in the success and affection she met. Qasim Bey Fahmi was so madly in love with her that this became his dominant passion. He pursued her affections without regard to

178

rank, family, or children. He spent so much money on her that she was the ornament of every gathering thanks to her beauty and attire. This was a life! On the other hand, to sit at home and wait for either of her two men—that was more than she could bear. Moreover, she felt the emptiness and ennui of a young woman whose heart has been deprived of love. She did not love the bey; his amazing charm no longer dominated her. Chances are that his charm evaporated when she discerned his treachery. She may well have harbored some rancor and resentment toward him. She was, however, very attentive toward him, lest her "sacrifice should have been in vain." Since she was a young woman of a practical bent, she deposited her past on the road to forgetfulness and turned her back on it, ignoring the occasional impact it made on her heart. The past and its handsome symbol— Ali Taha—were two milestones that would never return. She focused her attention on her husband, since he was her life partner as well as her current and future companion and since life had demanded of him—as of her—a hideous sacrifice. He too—like her—was focused on a single goal. In addition to all this, he was a young man who could love her and provide her with a happy married life. She encouraged his attempts to promote their mutual happiness, sharing a drink with him, exchanging kisses, and hoping that their playacting would mature into a genuine life. Had Ihsan's nature merely been carnal she would have achieved all the happiness she craved. Her heart, however, still yearned for affection and love that she didn't find in the pleasure and luxury her life afforded her. For this reason she continued to feel empty and bored. The more this feeling plagued her, the more ardently she embarked on her life of merriment and opulence, till she surpassed even her husband's aspirations.

She normally left home every morning once her husband went to work. She felt such an aversion for the apartment that she could not abide to stay there alone. Her favorite destinations were major stores, where she cruised past their displays, made her way down their crowded aisles, and perhaps purchased something she needed, ignoring the young men who ventured to flirt with her. What need did she have for a new man when she had two at home? Besides, her heart kept telling her that she would eventually adjust to her husband, fall in love with him, and emerge from all her anxiety. When ennui did chance to get the better of her and she felt disgusted, she might forget discretion and remember her life's shortcomings (her parents, her fall, and her present life). Then a rebellious surge would sweep through her and her soul would tell her to pursue pleasure to the limit. But she would not succumb. She burned no bridges in such circumstances, differing in this respect from Mahgub. She puttered about each morning like a man out of work. Perhaps she would catch a tram or bus for a return trip to an outlying suburb. One day she learned that a friend of hers was moving soon to Rome where her husband would serve with the legation. This news had an amazing effect on her. She felt like touring all the countries of the world. Such an active life would be a fitting way for a worried person to forget his woes and to pull down a thick curtain over life's banality. She told Mahgub, once she had shared this news, "How delightful it would be to travel to Rome!"

He asked her with astonishment, "Do you really want to travel?"

"Yes, why not?"

With a smile on his lips, he inquired, "What about the bey?"

"Perhaps he'll extend this favor to me later on."

He grasped what she meant by "later on." Shrugging his shoulders he said, "If his passion ever flags, he'll do nothing at all."

Their eyes met in a moment of shared realization. He wished to exploit this propitious opportunity to the full and commented, "At present he yields to your every desire. So don't let this lovely opportunity escape you. Such a happy break only comes once in a lifetime. Forget this sudden desire to travel, for it's a fantasy. Remember that if you lose his love one day, life will become a dreary, glum affair. If we don't make the best of our current circumstances, in the future we'll be forced to leave this neighborhood for an impoverished one. Then refined society will surely close its doors in our faces and we'll become the target of witty laughter. So we need to plan carefully for the long term."

Reflecting briefly on what he had said, he realized that he had spoken with the easy nonchalance of a pimp. He was delighted by this, counting it a manifest victory for his philosophy and willpower. Ihsan thought for a long time about what he had said and was soon convinced of the wisdom and farsightedness of his comments.

37

ugust arrived and he drew the first payment of his government salary, which was beyond anything he had even dreamed of during his days of starvation. It truly was amazing that he was not delighted by it. He was, however, beset by cravings as his desires multiplied and his life became an insatiable, importunate fire. The payment reminded him of his parents who were waiting eagerly their cut. His father's indemnity payment had no doubt run out. Perhaps he was now selling household furniture as he himself had done last February. His father would definitely be unable to pay the rent for his dwelling. Perhaps his parents now lacked shelter or food. What could he do?

He had surely been wise when he decided to conceal his appointment from his parents. He had taken precautions about the matter, asking al-Ikhshidi not to say anything about it in al-Qanatir, to prevent anyone from learning about it until the appropriate moment, but when might that be? His salary did not suffice for the expenses of this fancy living. He realized that it was inadequate to pay for the necessary show. If he sacrificed two or three pounds to his parents, his budget would be compromised, he would be disgraced, and his hopes would be shattered. How could he cope with these difficulties? Anger gripped him. He always grew angry when anxious or perplexed—as if he believed deep down that there was nothing worth being anxious or perplexed about. In spite of himself, however, he remembered his parents as they appeared in his mind's eye. He saw his father in his sickbed—but this image didn't trouble him much—and his mother with her weak eyes, dreadful silence, and profound belief in him and his future. He tried to flee from her and to banish her from his mind, but to no avail. So he resolved to vanquish vehemently and rudely the emotion these images caused him. Love for his parents was not his main reason for thinking about them. Instead it was his feeling of responsibility toward them. He had grasped this fact from the outset, and this was one reason for his increased anger. Did his soul still retain such fantastic notions? What did filial duty mean? Wasn't this a silly custom associated with the social construct of the family? Yes, indeed! He would jettison this idea the same way he had previously rid himself of other related notions. He would care only for himself, his glory, and his pleasure. He wondered why they were still alive. What use were they? What meaning did their lives have? Why didn't they die, enjoy eternal peace, and leave other people in peace too? Filial piety turned into an evil once it limited a son's happiness. Indeed, everything that interfered with an individual's happiness was evil. That was self-evident. He believed this profoundly, but what was he to do? Should he sever every tie with al-Qanatir and allow his parents to fend for themselves? How could he marshal the funds they needed? The truth was that he couldn't spend anything on them. It was equally apparent that he would be unable to forget them.

❋

He continued to feel worried and pensive till he left the ministry. He had reached no decision, even if his feeling of selfishness had not triumphed. At Qasr al-Aini Street he ran into Mr. Ahmad Badir, who was coming out of the newspaper's headquarters. They shook hands warmly and Mahgub was immediately overwhelmed by the fear he felt whenever he remembered this terrifying friend. They walked along, side-by-side, chatting the way they once had on the road to the university and in the Orman Gardens. The young journalist asked him how he was and about his job and Qasim Bey. He also commented on the difficulties of his life as a journalist. Then Mahgub, as if wanting to flatter him, said, "Journalism is a deadly serious art. Compared to it, government positions are fun and games."

Ahamd Badir replied delightedly, "You're so right, dear friend. That's why it astonished me that a young man not unlike us should forsake his government position and leave a respectable career to struggle in the field of journalism."

"Really?" Mahgub stammered as an inquisitive expression appeared on his face.

"Yes. I'm referring to our friend Ali Taha."

His protruding eyes became anxious. He frowned but cloaked his concern with astonishment as he exclaimed, "Ali Taha!"

Ahmad Badir replied, "He's a daring young idealist and quickly became frustrated with the university library. He has agreed with some of our classmates to publish a weekly magazine advocating social reform."

"What about his master's degree?"

Ahmad Badir replied, "He told me, 'Let's leave research to researchers and focus our attention on something grander. Let's devote all our effort to transforming Egypt from a nation of slaves to a nation of free men.'"

Mahgub Abd al-Da'im's face was expressionless for a time as

he reflected. Then he said, "The fact is that Mr. Ali Taha has a practical bent rather than a talent for abstract thought."

Eying him critically, the journalist said, "And that's to his credit! Both temperaments, although different, are lofty ones. The truth is that our friend is a sincere and zealous young man. He's renounced a comfortable life to advocate his ideals, even though this will mean hardship and risk for him. The principles our friend believes in are not ones that provide a journalist much cover. Fools may contest them and bigots may attack them. Perhaps it will be worse than that. What should someone advocating belief in science, society, and socialism expect?"

Mahgub did not respond. Instead he asked, "Has the magazine appeared yet?"

"The first issue will come out early this month."

After some hesitation, Mahgub inquired, "Where did he get the money for a project like this?"

"His father gave him a hundred pounds."

Mahgub asked a bit sarcastically, "Does his wealthy father believe in socialism?"

Ahmad Badir laughed and replied, "Perhaps he considers the magazine an investment. He's done his part to help out, and now its fate is up to his son."

Mahgub shook his head and said in a somewhat disparaging tone, "In the hostel Ali Taha told us about his principles time and again, and conversation like that is a pleasant way of spending an evening, but for a man to quit his job and make a career of discussing his principles—an act that could lead him to prison dungeons—is conduct of which the least one can say is that it's insanity. Our friend isn't crazy; so how could he have done this? Look at our friend Ma'mun Radwan and how he kept talking about Islam. Then see how he's traveling off to Paris to prepare for a grand career as a professor. There's a wise young man."

185

Ahmad Badir retorted in a tone that revealed his astonishment, "Ma'mun Radwan is also a sincere young man. I assure you that he will finish his studies with distinction, as always, and will doubtless become a Muslim imam."

"I have my doubts."

Badir shrugged his shoulders but did not contest his friend's claim because they were drawing near to Ismailiya Square, where they would need to part. He simply observed, "Mr. Ma'mun got married yesterday, and the newlyweds will travel abroad at the end of this month."

Here the first lines of these diverging lives were being drawn on the wide page of the world. No one knew how they would extend in the near and distant future or what varieties of luck and fate awaited the respective parties. All he knew was that any of these lives, except for his, could be publicized by a narrator like Ahmad Badir. For his life story to be made public would constitute a scandal. He could care less about this, but it meant he had to beware of untoward consequences—like anyone who lived surrounded by idiots and fools. He could not afford to feel overconfident or to dismiss too lightly the catastrophe that could befall him. It was amazing that although he and Ali Taha were exact opposites, it was entirely possible that society would throw both of them into a dungeon, making no distinction between the former who worshiped the status quo and the latter who rejected it. When they reached the square, they heard newspaper vendors hawking their wares and touting a meeting of the ruling party. Remembering something, Mr. Badir said, as he shook hands, "That reminds me. The prime minister has lost the palace's confidence."

Mahgub was disturbed, because he recalled that Qasim Bey Fahmi was a prominent figure in the current alliance. He asked, "How about the English?"

The young man grimaced and said, "The High Commissioner's affections have shifted." The two young men parted, and Mahgub headed for Sulaiman Pasha Street, frowning and depressed. This new concern, however, rescued him from the anxiety that had overwhelmed him since he received his salary. Faced by this looming danger, he no longer hesitated to decide about his parents. They were the first victims of the political crisis.

38

He brought the news to his wife. They conversed at the table and then on the balcony. They both wondered whether Qasim Fahmi would keep his post or fall with the government. The bey was one of those members of the current regime known for infighting. Thus there was no hope he could stay on should the cabinet resign. Mahgub commented, "If the bey is pensioned off, I'll definitely be transferred to some obscure position—unless I'm banished to the most rural district—and my long-range hopes will become impossible—if I'm not fired outright."

Had he struggled this hard only to meet such a sad fate? Was this the reward for his audacity, spirit of adventure, and contempt for everything? Filled with sorrow and grief he began to gaze at his wife with eyes that saw nothing. Ihsan was no less sad and glum than he. She also brooded about the future, imagining what she might expect. She was not much concerned about a deflation of long-term dreams but was oppressed by the jolt to her current security. Would she actually lose this luxurious, comfortable life?

Would the spring that provided water for her thirsty family run dry? Would she find herself some day in one of those rural towns as a dingy home's mistress whose life revolved around caring for it and tending to its master? These notions were more like nightmares. She did not know how she could face them on the morrow if they became real. It was clear, however, that this information was premature, for there was no echo of it in the newspapers, which they began to read carefully. Many of their friends declared that the time had not yet come. The days of August passed quietly, one after the other, till their feeling of confidence returned. Indeed Mahgub remembered his parents and wondered what he should do about them. This time with resolute determination he wrote his father a letter in which he expressed his sorrow at being unable to assist him. He stated that he was still looking for work and promised relief soon. He told himself, to clear his conscience, that the man could wait another month or two till he could assist him under more favorable circumstances. But his peace of mind did not last. The news that Ahmad Badir had announced resurfaced at the beginning of the next month. So many rumors were flying that the air was full of them. The horizons continued to presage impending disaster. The couple returned to their reflections as various fears gripped them.

Mahgub met with his boss Salim al-Ikhshidi in his office one day to ask what was happening. He found the man as calm and collected as ever. Mahgub was not unduly swayed by this calm and composure, because he knew for a fact that al-Ikhshidi would not relinquish these even in a crisis. When the man's round eyes looked up at him inquisitively, the young man, who was still standing, asked, "What are the facts behind these rumors that are on every tongue?"

In a voice that had lost not an iota of its authority, al-Ikhshidi asked, "What rumors?"

"That the government will fall. What's behind them?"

"Whatever is," al-Ikhshidi replied with a smile.

"Is it really possible for this alliance to end?"

Swept up by a mischievous desire to torment him, al-Ikhshidi replied, "Everything is transitory."

Mahgub, who was so infuriated and enraged by the man's frigid demeanor that he was forced to hide his feelings behind a smile, said, "Your Excellency doubtless knows many things."

Since his soul would not allow him to deny this, he smiled mysteriously and said confidently, "Just be patient. Perceptive people will not have long to wait."

"How about a reassuring comment?"

As his desire to torment Mahgub returned, he asked, feigning ignorance, "What's scaring you?"

The young man's bulging eyes widened in astonishment and he raised his eyebrows. Then he retorted sarcastically, "Aswan's beautiful in August!"

Al-Ikhshidi shrugged his shoulders dismissively and replied, *"Any place glory flourishes is fine."*

"So the rumors are well-founded then."

Al-Ikhshidi was silent for a moment while he searched for an answer that would not make him look like a fool in the near future or thereafter. Then he said, "No one knows even now; beyond that, well, politics is crazy."

Enraged and resentful Mahgub returned to his office, telling himself: Mrs. Umm Salim's son wants me to think he's an astute politician. Damn him!

At noon, the ministry was filled with the rumor that the cabinet actually had resigned. Someone said he had telephoned Bulkeley and that the report had been confirmed. The office workers were agitated in a way seen only when cabinets fall. They congregated in the corridors speaking in raised voices about the new ministers.

Mahgub was very upset and there was a glum look in his eyes. The messenger came to tell him that Qasim Bey had left the ministry. He contacted al-Ikhshidi by phone to ask which direction the bey had been heading when he left. He replied he didn't know. Mahgub spoke with a bunch of friends in the different ministries—by telephone—and received these responses. "What news do you have, so-and-so?" "The situation is critical. What's the latest news, sir?" "Shit. Anything new, so-and-so?" "They hit the one-eyed man's good eye. Have you heard the strange rumors, my dear?" "About the cabinet? To hell, sir." And so forth, until he felt certain that the cabinet was in its final throes.

His telephone rang, and it was his wife, Ihsan. He felt apprehensive. "Have you heard the news?"

"The cabinet?"

"Yes. It resigned."

"How do you know?"

"A special edition of the newspapers."

"So . . . ."

"I'm calling to reassure you."

"How? This doesn't make sense."

"No, it makes a lot of sense. I'll give you the details when you come home. For now, you should know that the bey told me the new cabinet will be different but that the alliance remains intact."

"You're certain?"

"I have some other news that will delight you. You'll hear it when you return."

She hung up, and then the young man immediately rose and left the room. On the way home he heard newspaper vendors proclaiming as loudly as possible the fall of the government. Interest and excitement were in the air everywhere. Despotism was routed, the bloodshedder had been toppled, and the rope of tyranny had been removed from the necks of the Egyptians, or almost. No one felt the delight he did, and had it not been for the good word from his wife he would have burst into tears. He found Ihsan waiting for him. She received him with a sweet smile and proceeded to tell him her news. She repeated in person what she had said over the telephone and then asked him, "Do you know who your new minister is?"

He asked her in amazement, "Who?"

"Qasim Bey Fahmi."

He stared at her dumbfounded, blushed, and then asked her, "Did he tell you that?"

"Yes."

He was overwhelmed by a feeling of relief and delight, but that did not last long. He was soon picking at his left eyebrow as he said, "Minister! I wish he had kept his current post. A cabinet post is a transitory thing, not a life appointment. Who will be there for us tomorrow?"

But his suspicion had no effect on her. She imagined that the cabinet post was her own. She replied incredulously, "He's the minister. Don't you understand?"

"Yes, darling. It's a happy opportunity. It's just that cabinets are as short-lived as happy dreams. It will resign sooner or later and then we'll find ourselves without a patron or at the mercy of merciless enemies."

She did not respond. He communicated his infectious anxiety to her, and she secretly cursed it. Thinking quickly and with penetration, the young man began to weigh matters and their possibilities. Then he said, "This is our last chance. So either we know how to exploit it and we're on easy street or we let it slip from our hands and are disgraced."

Their eyes met. She grasped what he meant but waited till he explained his idea. Mahgub continued, "If he resigns when we're in a reasonable position, we won't have to regret his resignation."

Then after a short silence, he concluded, "I must join his office staff."

"As his secretary?"

He shook his head as if to say, "That wouldn't suffice." He continued, "His secretary is at the sixth level, which is useless, but his officer manager is at the fourth level."

"Is it possible to leap from the sixth to the fourth level?"

"I could be promoted to fifth in lieu of fourth. In the civil service there are interpretations broad enough to allow anything. What do you think?"

She bit her lip to hide her proud smile. She understood that any level to which he ascended was tantamount to hers. She entertained no doubt that the hoped-for fourth level could preserve her at the standard of living she currently enjoyed. She sincerely shared his feelings and stammered in a low voice, "I don't think he would refuse me any request."

So he responded enthusiastically and supportively, "Go for it. Go for it, champ! Our destiny rests on the result of your efforts."

The next morning he picked up *al-Ahram* with interest and looked at the front page. He ran his eyes down a column of photographs, pictures of the new ministers, and found what he was looking for in the middle: a picture of Qasim Bey Fahmi. So his eyes rested on it, and he sighed deeply. Was it possible that his hope would be realized? Could a kiss, a look, or a sigh transport him from one status to another and promote him from one rank to the other?

39

Within a few days the new minister had taken up residence in Cairo—rather than Bulkeley—because of chronic asthma. On the fourth day after the bey's appointment as minister, Mahgub learned that a decision had been made to choose him for the position of office manager. Ihsan greeted him with a smile and said proudly, "Congratulations!" His heart pounded with delight, and he was bowled over by the surprise—as if he had not focused his entire attention on this hope for the past four days. The aspiration had turned into a splendid reality. He would become a senior government official. The fifth level wasn't anything to scoff at. So what if it was a stepping stone to the fourth? In his mind's eye he could see the fourth boldly inscribed. Then the words evolved into images: an armchair surrounded by assistants as many people of all classes approached deferentially. Had he been able to see himself imagining this glory, he would have been as scornful as ever, because he was frowning haughtily and casting a lofty gaze around from a supercilious head. At that time he took pleasure in flipping through the pages of his recent past: those February nights, the ful shop in Giza Square, the trip to the Pyramids, his comings and goings between Giza, al-Fustat Street, and al-Ikhshidi—his hand extended to beg—his marriage, and then this culmination! His head, which was crammed full of daring and philosophy, seemed a lamp illuminating the right path. So he felt good and rubbed his hands together gleefully.

He went to the ministry early the next day and sat in his office, which he was about to quit and which seemed rather mean. He was, however, not the only person to arrive early. The door opened and Mr. Salim al-Ikhshidi appeared on his doorstep. He felt uncomfortable but naturally did not allow his discomfort to show on his face. He rose smiling to welcome his guest. He was wondering what had inspired the man to swallow his pride and come to his office. Holding his hand out to him with delight, he said, "Welcome, Your Excellency. Come in and have a seat!"

They both sat down. Al-Ikhshidi volunteered one of his rare smiles and spoke in general terms about the new cabinet and the bey who would replace Qasim Bey. Then with his customary composure he said, "I have something I want to disclose to you. I've instructed your messenger not to allow anyone to enter."

The young man guessed what he wanted to say and felt spiteful and resentful but in his welcoming, delighted tone said, "That's fine. Here I am at your command."

Al-Ikhshidi focused his round eyes on him and said, "The matter is deadly serious since it concerns our future and we definitely both stand to profit from it. But I would like to ask you first of all: Haven't you found me to be a sincere friend?"

"Of course, the best of friends."

Mahgub said that, feeling amazed by this pleasant, gracious tone, which he had not heard al-Ikhshidi use before. What had become of all the commanding, forbidding, and scolding? Where were the coldness and the haughtiness? He felt deep inside intrusive resentment and scorn. Then he heard him say, "Thank you. Our friendship is a precious treasure. Because of it we will be able to plunge into any difficulties like a hand in a glove."

"As always, what you suggest is the wisest approach."

He secretly observed: You may speak as much as treachery requires about friendship. Cunning devil, I know you as well as you know yourself. It's enough for me to understand myself to understand you. Every bane has its corresponding nemesis!

Al-Ikhshidi gave him a piercing look and said, "I've learned that a memo is being drafted to appoint you the minister's office manager."

This was the essential point. Did he want him to relinquish the post to him? How stupid he was! How could he have forgotten that Mahgub was his pupil? Religion, morality, and etiquette could not keep him from this position. Did the man think that his "friendship" would succeed where all other powers had failed? He said calmly, "Yes. I learned that only yesterday."

Al-Ikhshidi replied, "This pleases me as it does you, although I would like to direct your attention to the fact that the office manager position is at the fourth level and you're at the sixth. If a fifth level had been vacant, you would have achieved your objective. If you take my position and let me have your new job, that will realize all our hopes."

Mahgub wondered privately whether al-Ikhshidi was a numbskull or just pretending to be one. Didn't he realize that he was aspiring to the fourth level itself? And suppose that a leap to the fourth level wasn't feasible for him, was there any doubt that he would rather have both of them at the fifth level than have al-Ikhshidi pave the way for his eventual promotion? Looking at his companion with pretended concern, he asked, "What do you want me to do?"

Al-Ikhshidi said, "Tell the minister that you would be satisfied with my position."

The critical moment had arrived. He realized that the friendship myth they had chanted in unison doubtless hung on a single word. He hesitated a little, remembering that al-Ikhshidi's enmity was not something to be dismissed lightly, since he was not a man like Ali Taha or Ma'mun Radwan whose vengeance would be limited by their honor. This was a man—just like him—who had no morals and no principles and who knew everything. What could he do? He reflected for a time. He told himself his secret would certainly come out some day, if people like Ahmad Badir did not actually know it. And what effect had Badir's mocking comments about the heroes of the party of the Society for Blind Women had on them? Tuzz! Then he shouldn't hesitate. Let al-Ikhshidi and his friendship go to hell. As a storm of disdain swept through him, he said, "Don't you think, Salim Bey, that this would mean rejecting an honor that the minister has chosen for me?"

Al-Ikhshidi cast him a look that seemed to say, "You son of a bitch!" With amazing self-control, though, he retained his composure. He was silent for a moment. He was ready to ask him to reconsider. One of his smiles was almost traced on his lips as graceful comments were lining up on his tongue. He almost said something about friendship and cooperation, but his will prevented all this. So he remained silent as his face and regard froze. He confined his commentary to asking in an expressionless voice, "Is that what you think?"

Mahgub replied nonchalantly after his guardian demon had gained the upper hand, "Yes. Don't you agree with me?"

Turning his eyes away, al-Ikhshidi muttered, "That makes sense. You're right. Thanks. Congratulations!"

He quit the room with unhurried steps, his pride having returned. Mahgub rested his elbows on his desk thoughtfully.

He had previously lost Ali Taha and Ma'mun Radwan and had quickly forgotten. This time he was assailed by fear. Enraged by this fear, he clenched his fist angrily. Apparently wishing to forget his concern, he rose and left the room for the personnel office to see for himself the memo of his appointment.

40

M r. Mahgub Abd al-Da'im—henceforth to be known as Mahgub Bey Abd al-Da'im—settled into the room reserved for the office manager. The senior staff of the ministry came in a delegation to congratulate him. It was a great day of memorable glory. Some of them congratulated him "in anticipation" on his promotion to the fourth level, as if it were a done deal. Salim al-Ikhshidi, however, did not come to offer his felicitations and thus frankly declared his enmity. News made the rounds in the ministry that al-Ikhshidi would transfer to Foreign Affairs, where he would be promoted to the fourth level. It was not difficult for Mahgub to guess the source of this rumor. He did not, however, discount its validity, because he knew of the man's links to leading statesmen. He told himself: Al-Ikhshidi's powerful—there's no dispute about that. Had it not been for my wife, I wouldn't have defeated him. He would have my place today. He felt delighted. If al-Ikhshidi really did transfer, that would clear the air for him and he would become the minister's right-hand man just as his wife was already tops with the minister.

Although he was no doubt overjoyed by this, his joy did not last long. He began brooding again about al-Ikhshidi's anger and the forms his revenge might take. Soon his spirit of scornful contempt resurfaced and his good humor returned. He began to tell himself: People love appearances and are deceived by dissimulation. If he was forced to defend himself, he would provide them with all the deceptive surface gloss they wanted, even if he were obliged to join the Society for Muslim Youth, for example. So tuzz for everything, except not for people, at least not in public. He was incapable of banishing al-Ikhshidi and his anger from his mind, however. He had a thought that troubled him greatly. Why hadn't this occurred to him before? Al-Ikhshidi was a former neighbor from al-Qanatir. Wasn't it possible that his desire for vengeance would be so great that he would spill the secret in some manner to his parents? He swallowed with difficulty and his face turned a pale yellow. He started to tug at his eyebrow with pensive discomfort. He remained thoughtful and uncomfortable until he realized that he should not sacrifice his joy on this glorious day to whispered insinuations that might never materialize. He snorted with resentful rage, clenched his fist angrily, and told himself: The course has been set. What's done is done. So let the results be what they may. It was quite a remote possibility that al-Ikhshidi would tell the truth about his marriage, because he himself knew facts about him that were no less damning. Moreover, al-Ikhshidi was too judicious to disclose a secret that would expose himself to Qasim Bey's wrath. On the other hand, he should anticipate that his father would hear about his appointment. He had better arrange to provide for the man's needs and to safeguard his honor. Wishing to shake off his concerns, he spread a piece of paper on his desk and wrote down the sum of his new salary: twenty-five pounds. His protruding eyes rested on the figure till he beamed. He would receive that much on the first of October, which was not too far off. Could the owner of the beanery in Giza Square imagine that? Indeed, not even Ma'mun Radwan himself would earn more after he returned from studying abroad—in eight years! Tuzz had scored a dazzling victory! He felt such relief at this realization that it consoled him for all the pain, discomfort, anxiety, and grief he had suffered. He felt a pure delight at his liberation from this imaginary but malignant malady called conscience or remorse. He did fear people at times, and jealousy tormented him on other occasions, but remorse was quite a different kettle of fish. His rejection of society and its values was dazzlingly complete. He certainly believed he would continue to be powerful and free to the end and that he would not soften or weaken even if stricken by ill health or forced to live in reduced circumstances. How beautiful it was to taunt death when dying and to stare at annihilation with an eye capable of processing what was happening without any terror about some imaginary force or nugatory god. In this way a free intellect could vanquish blind instincts and trumped-up superstitions. He recalled Qasim Bey Fahmi, al-Ikhshidi, and tens of others with whom he was in contact in his new life. All of them seemed to belong to his school. No—he haughtily rejected that idea. Those men did evil knowing it was evil. Some committed an act without distinguishing between good and evil. Others simply did not take the trouble to reflect. Some did evil believing it to be good. He was unlike all the others, because he denied the existence of both good and evil and spurned the society that had concocted them. He believed in himself and nothing else. Some things were pleasant or painful, useful or harmful, but good and evil were purely pointless fantasies. Many a person would say, "If everyone believed that, everyone would perish." That was true. There was no debate about that. But he wasn't a big enough fool to seek converts to his point of view, which he reserved for himself alone. If he did speak, it would be to men like himself who were liberated from those idiotic believers. Society tolerated people who were good at concealment—like him. Since society was only interested in its continued existence, it was hostile even to its well-wishers who sang about perfecting it—people like Ali Taha and Ma'mun Radwan. Society resembled a conceited woman who spurns any admirer she finds criticizing her. Thus society's critics are destined to fatigue, struggle, and perhaps even prison.

Life was good. Then, remembering something, he corrected himself, "Except for one thing." That was Ihsan or the tyrannical emotion that appears only with love. Where was love? The young woman shared his hopes and was a model spouse, but he felt she was conscientiously performing a duty. She resembled an employee who loves the profession rather than the job itself or who doesn't love or hate it. She had tied her destiny to his and loved life the way he did. She was as fond of luxury as he was. But something was missing that kept their relationship from being totally perfect. This deficiency alarmed him even during those brief moments when they both seemed tipsily happy—lip to lip and breast to breast. The missing thing was important, even if he would say of it in the throes of despair: tuzz! Indeed it provoked a revolution inside him similar to the one hunger had once fomented. Thus he seriously thought he should do as he had been done by. Indeed, he toyed with the idea of renting a room and furnishing it, just in case. Who knew? Perhaps people would seek it out sooner or later. As he had given, so should he receive.

※

On the evening of that glorious day, friends streamed into the elegant apartment in the Schleicher Building to present their felicitations to the office manager's wife. During their conversation, which was merry and joyous, someone suggested they should all celebrate Mahgub's promotion. One man, addressing Ihsan, remarked, "Next Thursday is the middle of the Islamic month and the full moon will be enthroned in the sky. Many folks will be heading downriver to al-Qanatir. What do you think about a moonlit cruise?" At this juncture he glanced discreetly at Iffat and continued with a wink of his eye, "And Iffat Bey has a beautiful little yacht."

Iffat was beside himself with joy, since his admiration for Ihsan was increasing day by day. He agreed with an alacrity that spoke for itself: "The yacht and its owner are at your command!"

The moment Mahgub heard the name al-Qanatir, a cold tremor pulsed through his body. Knowing also that the friends' enthusiasm was not directed at him in person, he objected, "This moonlit excursion isn't appropriate for September's cold, damp weather."

Iffat laughed. Fearful that this golden opportunity might elude him, he said, "It's obvious that your important position has infected you with some senior-citizen bug that makes you shake even in nice weather."

In other circumstances, this praise couched as blame would have pleased Mahgub. His alarm, however, did not allow him to enjoy it. He argued vigorously, "It's a big world. Choose any place you want, but as for al-Qanatir . . . ."

So many objected that the rest of his statement was lost. He did not know how to convince or dissuade them. Faced by their protests, he felt overruled.

Meanwhile Iffat began, "It's pointless to object. The best thing would be for you to listen to _____. The yacht will be at Qasr al-Nil at the time you all specify. A charming buffet and one bottle of whiskey for every three people. Let me count you."

The roar of approval mounted and Ihsan joined in their delight. Mahgub started glancing anxiously at their faces, a meaningless smile inscribed on his lips. There was no way for him to opt out of this trip to al-Qanatir. He would stroll through the gardens there in the moonlight. Wasn't it likely that he would encounter a resident who knew him? Yes, indeed; this was likely. Therefore the best thing he could do was to find some excuse for staying on the yacht. Yes, he could not resist the rowdy, obstinate fun-lovers. So he would go, because he was forced to. At any rate the gardens were far removed from the train station, far from the dilapidated, miserable abode.

41

For four days he derived pure enjoyment from his important position. All the employees—junior and senior staff—who came in contact with him sensed that he was a presumptuous official who would have to be accorded his due in full measure, who would pardon no error, and who spoke only to command. The more accommodating his staff members became—and they had no choice about this—the more extreme and despotic he was. He enjoyed this aggressive despotism so much that he would at times have liked to spend his entire day at the ministry, commanding and scolding.

Then it was Thursday, the appointed time for the excursion. The couple left their home and proceeded toward Qasr al-Nil. As they walked along, Ihsan muttered, "You're perhaps the only member of the group who doesn't own a car!"

Laughing, Mahgub replied, "Slow means safe."

Her comment, however, prompted him to flag down a taxi, even though they did not have far to go. Thinking of her grumbling tone, he commented sarcastically to himself: It's shocking that

Uncle Shihata Turki's daughter doesn't have a car of her own. Then he remembered the burdens that his new life imposed on him like his desire to rent and furnish a room, budgeting a few pounds from his salary for his father, and his need for other luxuries and expenses. The matter frightened him. He commiserated with himself: No matter how long I live, I'll always be short of cash. They soon reached the yacht's mooring. Leaving the taxi behind them, they headed toward their waiting friends as the night's gloom descended on the horizons. They were warmly received. Iffat Bey came toward the couple, shook hands with them, and then offered his arm to Ihsan. She accepted and the pair led the first group onto the yacht. Mahgub did not like the yacht's owner. He had started to dislike him ever since accepting his invitation to the Fantasio. He could see in the man's handsome eyes telltale signs of infatuation with his wife. So he was annoyed, felt outraged, and glared at the other man's red hair, light complexion, and athletic body with angry, hate-filled eyes.

The vessel was small but beautiful and elegant. It had two levels. The lower held the cabins and the upper was a deck surrounded by a railing against which cozy seats were arranged in a circle. At the bow, they found tables covered with delectable edibles. Iffat Bey gave the order to hoist the anchor. So the yacht left its mooring and headed north, guided by the splendid moon at the center of the eastern horizon, where it was rising behind the palm trees. Thus the voyage began.

The friends, who sat facing each other, started to chat, enjoying the pleasant, moist air. Mahgub began to glance at the beaming faces and slender physiques. This array of youthful good looks dazzled him. He discovered that his wife was surrounded by a halo of admiration and admirers some distance away. He recalled the days when he admired her from the window of his room in the hostel, although he recognized that she was even more radiantly beautiful and enchanting now. He sensed the profound gulf that separated them. Quick, agitated images passed before his mind's eye. He saw Ali Taha both joyful and sad, Uncle Shihata Turki, the Minister, Salim al-Ikhshidi, and his own bedchamber in the Schleicher Building. He found himself wondering whether he would rather have Ihsan's heart and body for his own in a quiet, honorable, conjugal dwelling, even if that meant he was merely an inglorious, low-ranking government employee. He had no ready answer for this question. Yes, his ambition was as strong as his emotion. Indeed, his ambition possibly was the stronger, but what was the use of the comparison? To distract himself he glanced at the Nile and then looked up at the full moon, which was gradually rising higher and becoming more limpid. The darker the night became, the more luminous and radiant it was. He was not, however, the type of person entranced by nature's charms. He liked to say, "Rapturous love of nature spoils the intellect and, since the beginning of time, has been the source of superstitions that still shackle us." He remembered his friend Ma'mun Radwan, who would wake at dawn for prayer and devotions. He would gaze at the stars and recite in a loving voice, his clear eyes gleaming like bright stars, the Qur'anic verses, *By night when it descends* and *By the heavens and by the night star.* Did any of the young men and women present love nature? He scrutinized them but found them too preoccupied with personal matters to show any interest in the physical world.

He heard Miss Fifi suggest seductively, "Why don't we dance?"

Ali Iffat immediately replied, "Dance if you want to, but can you dance without music?"

Ahmad Asim piped up, "Here's good news. I've brought my accordion."

People exclaimed appreciatively and glanced about to search for a sweetheart. Ahmad Asim took out his instrument and began to play, swaying in his seat to the dance tunes. Everyone rose to dance, except for Ihsan and Mahgub, who did not know how to, and Iffat Bey, who chose to keep them company. They began to watch the dancers with silent admiration. Then Iffat Bey announced that he was skeptical about Ihsan's claim that she did not know how to dance. He encouraged Ihsan, "I'll teach you. This is something you need to know. What do you think?"

With her eyes fixed on the dancers, she stammered, "I don't know."

"A person who doesn't know how to dance will feel out of place at fancy balls. Don't you agree, Mahgub Bey?"

Mahgub sensed the danger encompassing him and wanted to evade it. So he remarked casually, "I don't think so. . . ."

Iffat laughed out loud and said, "What a nineteenth-century couple!"

Ihsan laughed along with him and said, "We may be your pupils one day."

The young man's eagerness showed in his face and gushing with delight he said, "Any time you want."

Mahgub said nothing. He was pretending to watch the dancers with interest while repressing his resentment and outrage. This idiotic young man, who was preoccupied by his own good looks, was preparing to assault his honor and would clearly act if he found an unguarded moment. Mahgub, however, was certainly going to deny him the opportunity. No fool like this was going to cause a new pair of horns to sprout on his head. He had volunteered his head for the golden horns, horns of glory and power. But how would she respond to this flirtation? Would this mysterious, fascinating young woman prove an easy target? He felt the fangs of venomous jealousy rip into his breast.

The dancing continued until Ahmad Asim grew tired or bored and stopped playing. Then the couples separated and returned to their seats with beaming faces. The full moon had risen into the heavens and its light had been appropriated by the Nile's undulating waters, which reflected it back and forth, sprinkling it around like pearls that ravished the eye.

Someone asked, "When can we start the buffet?"

A companion answered, "Not till the yacht is moored at the garden, you hungry scamp."

Someone else asked, "Why don't we play cards?"

Many people, however, objected to this suggestion, complaining that it would spoil the pristine character of the excursion. So they resumed their chatting. Mahgub was drawn out of his reflections by the voice of Mr. Husni Shawkat, who was saying, "How can it not be important? The Nazi Party's successful rise to power is a very grave matter."

Ahmad Asim protested, "But the personal prestige of President Hindenberg will most probably swallow Hitler."

"Look ahead. Don't you see that Hitler's in the prime of his youth while the president's at the end of his life?"

"Then the future holds a bloody war."

"That seems reasonable, although France won't wait for Germany to regain strength or prepare to pounce on it. There is a strong circle of states that are allied with France—like Poland, Czechoslovakia, and the Balkans. Don't forget that mighty Italy considers itself to be Austria's protector. If these nations make common cause—and perhaps Russia will join—the steel ring will slowly and gradually tighten till Germany is eventually strangled and annihilated."

"How about England? Would it look the other way while Germany is being strangled?"

"Why not?"

"England's too cunning to allow France—or any other country—to dominate Europe."

Mahgub listened to this conversation with interest. Despite his vast familiarity with domestic politics, he was sublimely ignorant of world affairs. He advised himself to pay attention to foreign news so he would be able to offer an opinion when appropriate. He pretended to be contemplating the moon, oblivious to his surroundings, to keep anyone from noticing his silence. He actually did lose the train of the conversation for some minutes. When his attention reverted to the session, he found talk had somehow switched to domestic issues. He heard one of them say, "Any ruler can subdue Egypt without any risk."

"As a matter of fact, any government established in Egypt becomes a dictatorship."

"This is a country where people say, 'I'm honored by your blow, sir.'"

Ahmad Asim stated categorically, "Egypt will never win its independence."

"It's used to being ruled by foreigners."

Iffat laughed and asked, "Why does Egypt need to be independent? Its leaders fight each other for power, and the people are unfit to govern themselves."

Mahgub thought this was a fitting opportunity to offer a moralizing comment in order to help shape a positive reputation for himself in line with a plan he had focused on since thinking about joining the Muslim Brotherhood. With a smile, he said, "Aren't you ashamed to say something like this about your own nation?"

Iffat laughed again and replied in a loud voice, "I don't have a drop of Egyptian blood in my veins."

His remark provoked a storm of laughter, but Mahgub's hatred for the man was doubled, not from chauvinistic anger but from disgust at his conceit. He remembered a ringing speech that Iffat's father had delivered in the Senate. Thinking he had a stranglehold on the young man, he said in a victorious tone, "So how do you explain the speech your father, the pasha, gave in the Senate during a budget discussion in which he defended the peasant in a magnificently nationalist fashion?"

Iffat guffawed and replied a bit sarcastically, "That was in the Senate. At home we both agree—my father and I—that the best policy for the peasant is the whip."

Everyone present—both men and women—laughed loudly. Mahgub smiled to mask his defeat. His fear had dissipated and he felt comfortable at being singled out as the defender of Egyptian nationalism. He told himself: Our true dress uniform is a cloak of hypocrisy. I won't abandon that! He wondered sarcastically: How do you suppose Ali Taha would reform these noble people? How would he implement his ideals?

With the passage of time the yacht progressed through the waves as if swimming through the resplendent light. Mahgub was roused from his thoughts a third time when a young man explained, "Doubtless the wife obliged her husband, the pasha, to move into a hotel while she retained the chauffeur."

A young woman asked with interest, "Did the pasha really make her choose between him and the chauffeur?"

"Yes."

"Which one did she pick?"

"The chauffeur."

He continued to listen selectively, to this person and that, feeling alert and attentive at times and absentminded and distracted at others, until al-Qanatir's gardens appeared in the moonlight like the sweetest dreams. Then all the friends rose eagerly as Iffat Bey invited them to the buffet.

42

hey rushed to be first to the tables and took their seats. Glasses were filled, and Iffat poured a glass for Ihsan. This was the first time she drank in public. In a low voice, she said, "One's enough for me."

The young man laughed and remarked, "You might as well cover yourself with a veil of piety and head down to al-Sayyida Zaynab's shrine to preach and counsel."

Then he whispered in her ear, "Look at Hikmat. She can drink an entire bottle without ever divulging a secret."

Ihsan saw that everyone was waiting for her to launch the party. So, she raised her glass a bit apprehensively and hands shot up with glasses to toast the office manager. Then they drained their glasses. Knives quickly sliced into the meat and forks pierced it to convey it to greedy mouths. The buffet area turned into a battlefield remarkable both for violence and delight as the casualties inflicted on food and drink multiplied. Ihsan noticed that Iffat Bey deliberately touched her each time he leaned forward to fill her glass and that his shoe had scuffed hers more than once—but she did nothing to encourage him. For his part Mahgub ate and drank voraciously, not because he felt like it but to escape from his emotions, since he had not stopped thinking about the house opposite the train station ever since the yacht anchored at the Barrages Garden quay. He was afflicted by a feeling of despair and fear he could not shake off. What might his parents be doing at that moment? Was his father still bedridden? What do you suppose his mother was doing? Had their money run out? Had they sold off some of the old furniture? Couldn't they have put to good use some of these tables' scraps? How could he free himself from this feeling of discomfort and despair? Who could help him train his emotions to obey the stern commands of his free intellect? He drank to excess and chattered on indiscriminately, making a good faith effort to evade his personal concerns and to impose himself on those around him, participating fully in the conversation. Someone asked the group of married couples whether marriage had lived up to their dreams. After exchanging anxious looks, the married couples burst into laughter. Another guest asked what the most enjoyable aspect of marriage was. A young husband replied, "It's love." Another said, "It's being rid of love!" A third volunteered, "Birth control!" Mahgub observed privately, "No, it's the golden horn!" Husni Shawkat volunteered for no apparent reason, "I lost fifteen pounds last week."

His fiancée exclaimed, "The rest next week!"

Ahmad Asim observed, "They say: unlucky at the gaming table, lucky at love."

A smiling young woman commented, "That's because someone who is an ill-starred gambler doesn't know how to cheat!"

Shawkat piped up again, "The strangest wager I ever witnessed was a young man who bet his sweetheart."

Everyone seemed interested, and many asked, "Really? How could that be?"

The inebriated young man answered, "He's a dear friend who once took his sweetheart to a private gaming club. He lost all his money, and eveyone had drunk so much they couldn't think straight. Then a drunk suggested that he should bet his sweetheart against all his losses. That way he would get all his cash back or lose his girlfriend. He accepted the proposal, made the bet, and lost his sweetheart."

"What did the woman think?"

"She was dead drunk. The winner acquired possession of her, or—put more accurately—she acquired possession of him."

"Who could that friend of yours be?"

"I can't tell you, because one of the parties is here."

Looks of disbelief were exchanged, mouths smiled skeptically, and curiosity showed clearly on every face—especially the women's. Ihsan asked Iffat Bey, "Who do you think the gambler is?"

Delighted by this question, the young man glossed it to fit his purposes, replying, "Only Mr. Shawkat knows that, and perhaps even he doesn't know."

"Do you approve of this type of wager?"

He responded with mock indignation, "I don't gamble with someone I love."

She realized that she had said more than was appropriate and resolved that her third glass would be her last. Many heads felt dizzy, and a couple began to quarrel, exchanging abusive comments. Mr. Husni Shawkat was almost delirious, and Mahgub Abd al-Da'im was drunk. Liquor had rewired his mind, allowing him to forget his cares and to dedicate himself eagerly to conversation and laughter.

Once the platters and bottles were empty, Iffat yelled at them, "To the garden!"

They echoed his call, "To the garden, to the garden," as they set off singly and in pairs. Mahgub wanted to stay behind on the yacht in keeping with his plan and stepped aside, even though he was severely intoxicated. He chanced to see, however, his wife leading the pack, arm-in-arm with Iffat Bey. His blood boiled and he clenched his teeth angrily. One of the brethren chanced upon him and took his arm, inviting him to walk with him. He did not resist, forgetting his resolve and fears. The garden was flooded with waves of sightseers—women and men. Some were walking and laughing together while others were seated, eating and drinking. These two varieties of fun-lovers spread merriment everywhere. Blissful harbingers and youthful bonds joined them all together harmoniously, not to mention their joyful love of mirth and jesting. Thus complete strangers struck up conversations and pelted each other with wisecracks without so much as a by-your-leave. They climbed a grassy hillock, descended a gully bordered by flowers, sheltered in a bower covered with jasmine and hyacinth-bean blossoms, or crossed a bridge over a creek that flowed silver in the moonlight, while the full moon peered down at them from the heavens' heights during its never-ending procession amidst the planets and stars, flooding the world with its brilliant light. Souls felt relaxed and pure. Anyone with a good voice began to sing, and musicians caused their strings to speak. The party from the yacht proceeded down the paths, creating an uproar and a din, and Mr. Husni Shawkat nonchalantly picked fights; so people stared at them. Mahgub, on his wife's right—Iffat Bey was beside her—was drunk. He was speaking and laughing, even though he was furious at the boy, who was sticking as close to his wife as her shadow. Despite his intoxication and jollity, he could not forget that he was in al-Qanatir, his hometown, and close to his wretched parents. He began to look around cautiously as he struggled to ward off the anxiety afflicting him. He considered heading back to the yacht more than once but kept yielding to the pull of his companions.

215

Then Husni Shawkat made them stop so he could buy figs from a vendor—an elderly man who hobbled along, so old and infirm that he leaned on a stick. Mahgub immediately thought of his father. When they continued on their way, the man's image stayed with him. His father, if he were able to leave his bed, would look just like this man, leaning on a stick at every step. He reflected for a time and then told himself: It's not unlikely that if his funds give out he'll pick up a basket of figs and roam the town with them. Perhaps he was struggling through the town somewhere with a basket of figs at that moment. He looked toward the train station as he staggered forward, feeling severely depressed. He no longer shared in his companions' amusement and delight. His good humor and joy had deserted him, and he felt anxious, sorrowful, and fearful. Coming here had been a big mistake. If he had stayed behind, however, would that have changed anything? If his father's estimate was accurate, he would have gone for three months without any support. What had the man done for himself and his mother? Given his weakness and ill health, how had he been able to confront life's severity? Three months or more: June, July, and August together with this week of September: in other words, the period when he had savored prosperity and the good life. His head felt heavy as his inebriation subsided leaving behind a hangover and a splitting headache. His audacity, which mocked everything, had betrayed him. So he wondered with alarm whether this awakening was what people call conscience. After the destructive rebellion that had characterized all his university life, after competing in this crucial trial that had lasted for three whole months and emerging with unequivocal success, how could his soul flounder in this despicable state of cowardice and pain? Clenching his fist violently and obstinately, he refused to admit that he felt lost and afraid, that the moan in his breast was his conscience, or that he still

216

could be moved by filial emotions. He refused all this stubbornly and furiously. To console and strengthen himself he dismissed his qualms as merely fear of a scandal that might threaten his social status. He did not pity his parents but was afraid their misery might induce them to upset his life and to cloud his glory's serenity. Their time would come on the first of October. When he received his new salary, he would purchase some peace of mind by sending his father a few pounds. Then he would be done with this torment. He repeated this notion to himself and affirmed it vehemently, attempting to recover his courage and ecstasy. When he noticed his surroundings once more, he found that he was stumbling about alone. Looking around blankly, he saw only Mr. Ahmad Asim. He asked him, "Where are our friends?" The man shrugged his shoulders, saying, "I don't know." Mahgub realized that he had lost the group. He felt tired and, suddenly, nauseous. Then he started vomiting. His companion took him by the hand and led him to the yacht and down to a cabin, where he stretched out on a bunk and fell asleep. He did not know how long he had been there, but in his imagination he kept seeing the fig seller till he imagined the man actually was his father, who had been forced by penury to accept the ignominy of begging.

43

hey were tired when they returned to the yacht and their voices were hoarse. The yacht set sail shortly before midnight. When Ihsan asked for her husband, Ahmad Asim said he was sleeping in a cabin. He offered to take her there, but Iffat volunteered instead. So, the two descended into the yacht's belly, where he preceded her down a side corridor to a cabin, opened the door, and stepped aside to make way for her. She entered, and he followed right behind her and closed the door. She found the cabin empty except for Ali Iffat's portrait on a table. She turned and saw the portrait's subject leering at her from the door with eyes that sang of passion and conquest. She realized that he had tricked her into his own cabin. Filled with fear, she asked, pretending she did not understand his designs, "Where's Mahgub?"

Smirking, with eyes red from drink, he suggested, "We'll go to him after a short rest."

In a grave voice she asked, "Why have you brought me here?"

His self-confidence was limitless. So he responded by kneeling before her, putting his arms around her legs, and embracing her.

Looking up at her, he said, "Don't ask, Ihsan. You know everything. In my condition, words would be a pointless repetition. Hasn't my heart been speaking since we first met? Hasn't it cried out so loudly tonight that I was afraid its pleas would reach the ears of our companions?"

Overwhelmed by anxiety and disapproval, she grasped his arms to shake them off her, shoved him away violently, and shouted at him in an angry, crude voice, "Please leave me alone. Leave me!"

Her face glowered with anger and she frowned. Witnessing her earnestness and aversion, he blushed with shame, allowed his arms to slacken, rose glumly without saying a word, and opened the door to allow her to leave the cabin. Then he showed her to her husband and withdrew. She found Mahgub sleeping or dozing. He was exhausted and his face was extremely pale.

※

The yacht docked at Qasr al-Nil around two a.m. The couple returned to the Schleicher Building in Ahmad Asim's car. Mahgub's head had cleared a little, but he was still tired and weak. The harm done to his spirit and psyche, however, was even more calamitous and bitter. His hangover had affected his spirit, leaving him depressed. Once his intoxication subsided, his soul was troubled, and he perceived the world with an invalid's senses. Ihsan disappeared briefly and returned with a cup of coffee for him. She sat facing him on the chaise longue and said, "You drank too much."

He acquiesced by bowing his head, although he recalled the other reasons that had troubled his peace of mind. He said irritably, "I never wanted to go on this excursion."

In defense of the trip, she replied, "What was the matter with it? It was an excellent, scenic excursion."

He snapped, "Mr. Iffat Bey's certainly a cad!"

Ihsan smiled and, after some hesitation, stammered, "It's over. I put a stop to it."

He leveled bulging, feeble, red eyes at her inquisitively. So she summarized what had happened. He insisted, however, on her telling him everything, no matter how trivial. Then she narrated the incident in minute detail. Finally he exploded, "Cad . . . scoundrel! But you handled it magnificently. What a vile bunch they all are."

His eyes flared, although he was wondering what right he had to criticize anyone in the world when he thought and acted the way he did. As if to answer himself, he remarked, "We can make fools of other people if we want but should never allow anyone to make a fool of us."

As she considered this remark, an enigmatic smile flitted across her lips. He began to think about his parents. His plan to lend them a helping hand in the interests of shaking any vexing shadow from his life was a sound one. He marveled at how a minor change in his body could deprive the world of its sparkle in the wink of an eye, transforming its pleasure and purity to such revolting pain and turbidity. Ihsan suggested that he should get some sleep, but he preferred to relax a little in the chair while she slipped into bed. He began to wonder again what he would do if this change persisted and he continued to see the world through a peevish convalescent's eyes. He trembled. He could find only one answer: suicide. That was how a devoted egoist would terminate his life. Even so, there were people in the world who preferred fatigue and torments over security—like his former friend Ali Taha. He had to admit they found some pleasure that was peculiar to them in their struggles, but what sort of pleasure was it? Was there really a pleasure associated with altruism and could it compare to egoism's? He admired that pleasure while also despising it. He could see Ali Taha's handsome face and recalled his zealous enthusiasm. He remembered his days in the hostel and Ma'mun Radwan. Then his head turned as if of its own volition toward the bed, and his eyes gazed at Ihsan, who was sound asleep. His memories were framed by astonishment and dreams.

44

He woke shortly before noon the next day—Friday—and at once memories of the previous night assailed him, bringing their sorrows with them. He got out of bed with ambitious vigor, bathed in cold water to restore body and soul, and entered the living room where he found his wife. She asked him tenderly, "How are you?"

Smiling in confused embarrassment, he mumbled, "Great . . . thanks to you."

He dressed and went out, making his way to Soult Parlour's garden café, where he met some fellow government officials. He drank a glass of lemonade, spent an hour chatting, left there, and allowed his feet to lead him from street to street, yielding to the pleasure of walking. Remembering the previous night, he frowned, appalled by the pain and despair he had felt and by the black thoughts and weak, submissive notions these had inspired. He was embarrassed by the mental and spiritual languor afflicting him and told himself: Up to now, I've triumphed thanks to my free intellect, forceful volition, and my lofty motto: tuzz. So I mustn't squander any of my hard-won treasure. Right, there were his high-ranking position, ambition and prestige, wine, women, good food and opulence—how could he allow a paralyzed father, morbid thoughts, and insane jealousy to spoil all these pleasures? He quickly recovered his energy and vitality as well as his ironic, heartless mentality. He greeted life once more with his customary audacity and boundless ambition. Everything seemed to be on track, as though life would continue to obey his logic forever. One Saturday, halfway through September, however, events showed him that even if he could control himself, he was incapable of controlling them.

Saturday was Qasim Bey Fahmi's time, and Mahgub was going to leave the apartment at seven p.m. sharp to afford his boss privacy, but the doorbell rang at six. The young man was not expecting anyone at that hour. He sauntered to the foyer to see who was there. The cook had opened the door, allowing him to see the visitor. He could not believe his eyes and began to stare with crazed confusion. He saw his father . . . his very own father, in the flesh. The man was standing at the threshold, leaning on a stick, casting a fixed, sullen look at him. Each of them stood nailed in place, their eyes rigid, not moving at all. Mahgub at that dreadful moment was overcome by fear, desperation, and an unprecedented sense of defeat. His father shattered the painful silence by saying in a voice that was weak but still capable of evincing his pain and fiery sarcasm, "Don't you recognize me anymore? Why don't you rush to welcome me?"

The young man shook off his daze and approached his father with shaky steps. He proffered his hand, which his father ignored. Mahgub said apprehensively and hesitantly, "Come in, father. Come in."

Leaning on his stick, the man entered, proceeding with heavy steps. His back was bent and his physique ruined. He began to examine the furniture and walls with an eye filled with ironic admiration. He said, "God! God! How intensely you must suffer from bitter misery and poverty, son."

Mahgub's apprehension increased and he felt devastated, for he could not utter a word. Here his father was terrorizing the apartment shortly before Qasim Bey arrived. These two facts he found to be irreconcilable. All the same, they were necessarily both facts, even if he hated to think of their consequences. How would he remember this fateful day on the morrow? Would he recall it as a dreadful crisis from which he had miraculously escaped or as a black day when all his dreams imploded? In his first rush of emotion, he could not think straight or devise any plan. The bedroom door opened just then, and Ihsan emerged. Perhaps the unfamiliar voice and commotion had prompted her to come out. She was amazed to find an elderly stranger there and cast a disparaging glance at his shabby appearance. Abd al-Da'im Effendi turned his head toward her, and a sad smile appeared on his lips. Turning matter-of-factly toward his son, he asked, "Your wife?" Then turning his head back toward her, he said, "Greetings to my son's wife. I'm your father-in-law, bride."

Ihsan stared at her husband's face and was distressed by his rigidity, anxiety, and despair. She observed in his eyes a hopeless look she had never seen before. All this confirmed for her the truth of the old man's claim. She knew nothing about the relationship between the two men or what her husband's position was but rallied to act appropriately. She approached the visitor and extended her hand to him respectfully, inviting him to sit down. Mahgub observed what was happening in front of him with dazed eyes, although he was progressing from negative befuddlement to positive bewilderment. He began to appeal to his willpower and intellect to extricate him from this predicament. As he started to awake from the impact of the surprise, he felt

uncomfortable that his wife was present and gestured unobtru-
sively for her to withdraw. She retired graciously at once. He worked
furiously to collect all his force to gain control of the situation and
to recover his mind and volition. The peril that threatened him,
drawing ever nearer with the minister's rendezvous, helped him
focus. Yes, he would have to hide his father soon from the visitor's
eyes and to deal with him in calm seclusion. The man was his
father no matter what, not a devil or fate or destiny. In a gentle,
tender voice, he said, "Come with me, father."

He offered his arm to the man, who did not refuse it, understanding that he wanted to speak to him in private. He rose with
his son's assistance, and Mahgub took him to the parlor to the
right of the entrance. Then he closed the door. His mind kept
wondering how his father had found his dwelling. Why had he
come? Was it entirely a coincidence that he had arrived on the
minister's day and shortly before his appointed time? He smelled
a rotten conspiracy, and al-Ikhshidi's ghostly image, with his
triangular face and round eyes, appeared to his mind's eye. A
tremor shot through his body, and his soul was filled with rancor
and hatred. Do you suppose he had told him the whole secret?
Good Lord, what catastrophe was stalking him? But no, his father
didn't know the fateful secret. Otherwise—being the rural, fiery
fellow he was—he would not have been able to stay calm. The
vile wretch had produced him at a fitting moment so he could
discover the truth himself. That way the shock would be more
atrocious. His forehead was dripping with cold sweat.

The man directed a fiery look at him and asked, "Why are
you standing in front of me that way. Why don't you welcome
me? Why don't you congratulate me on my recovery?"

The angry man fell silent to catch his breath. Then he continued in a harsh, ironic tone, "I've been so distressed by what I
understood to be your poverty, misery, and futile efforts to get a

job that I was moved to leave your mother by herself in al-Qanatir to come in person to console you. May God come to your aid, you poor darling."

Feeling somewhat reassured after closing the door, Mahgub was able to say, "Father, don't make fun of me. I know I deserve your wrath, but let me explain what may seem confusing. Then you be the judge."

"Is there any need to explain, son? Just by looking around I can see the penury of your existence."

Mahgub bit his lip and said, "By God, father, I've never forgotten you. By God, no opportunity to assist you has arisen that I have neglected. Despite these deceptive appearances, I've gone through some rough times. That's why I haven't been able to rest till I was reassured about you and my mother."

The scowl on the old man's face grew grimmer, and he snapped resentfully, "Rough times, dutiful son? What have you been waiting for in order to give us a couple of pounds? Are you waiting on a cabinet post? I'm amazed that you've been able to enjoy life while knowing that your parents are ravaged by want, hunger, and eviction. I begged you to help with tears in my eye, but now I know I was addressing a dead conscience. You left us to infirmity and poverty so that we've had to sell our household furniture, and here you are enjoying a high position, a large salary, and a cushy residence, but all you find in that is 'rough times' that won't allow you to rescue us from having to beg. Isn't that so, generous son?"

Mahgub's face was so pale it resembled a dead man's. He felt like a person strangling who vainly shudders and struggles to take a single breath. His father's words had not moved his heart but had confused and distressed him, placing him in a quandary. So he said, "Your words hurt me deeply, father. Listen to me. I'll tell you the truth and atone for my error. I'll lay to rest your

226

charges that I haven't been sufficiently dutiful. God knows I was going to tell you about my success and provide you with assistance the first of next month. I was given my position two months ago. Although penniless, I had to present a suitable façade, otherwise I would have lost a once-in-a-lifetime opportunity. So, I borrowed a large sum of money that I still haven't paid off. That's how I won the position while still suffering from embarrassment and want. That's the truth."

The man shook his head skeptically and resentfully. "You're too preoccupied by presenting an appropriate appearance, having an elegant residence, and fancy banquets."

Mahgub realized that al-Ikhshidi had spared no effort in defaming him. Struggling to contain his rancor and anger, he said, "These appearances, even if they seem luxuries, are pre-requisites for my position."

"Was leaving us to writhe in hunger a prerequisite for this glorious position?"

Exerting a death-defying effort to mask his anger and resent-ment, the young man said, "Of course not, father. I've clearly stated my good intentions. So don't hinder my effort with your grudges or deny me my chance at success."

"I assume that won't be achieved till you slay us."

"No, it will be achieved in a way that will make all of us happy."

Abd al-Da'im Effendi was silent for a time, staring at his son with skepticism and suspicion. Then he asked, "If that's how things are with you, how could you get married? Why didn't you postpone the marriage till you had some money? And how could you get married without telling us, not to mention asking our opinion?"

Mahgub felt relieved by this question from his father, since it showed that he did not know the fateful secret. In a soft voice, he said, "The marriage was the price of the position, as so often happens these days. I married into a respected family that's related to the minister, and the marriage was one of the reasons for my financial problems. Perhaps you've grasped now the difficult circumstances that have governed my life during the last two months."

Although the father was not satisfied and although the son's state of nervous tension and discontent had only intensified, each was planning to say something when the doorbell rang suddenly. The door opened and then closed. They heard heavy footsteps in the foyer, and Mahgub recognized them easily.

45

His heart pounded violently and a tremor of fear passed through his limbs without his being able to master it. The loathsome image of al-Ikhshidi loomed before his eyes once more. How was this night going to end? Would he remember it in the future with laughter or tears? His father too heard the visitor's footsteps and asked, "Were you expecting a guest?"

He replied without any hesitation, pretending to be nonchalant, "Yes, this is my father-in-law who has come to visit his daughter."

"Aren't you going to receive him?"

He stuttered and then said resolutely, "No, my wife will find an excuse to explain my absence. I'll introduce you to him some other time."

They fell silent. The old man sensed that his son was embarrassed to introduce him to his father-in-law and tucked in his chin quietly and sadly. Mahgub sat by the door trying his hardest to calm his nerves. He glanced stealthily and angrily at his father, revealing his resentment and rancor. The night had to end peacefully. He felt intuitively that if the night did end peacefully, he would have saved his life and hopes forever. But why should he be afraid? The minister had safely reached his destination, and his father's state revealed that he did not know the dreadful secret. All he had to do was to be patient and wait until the bey left—as he had arrived—peacefully. All the same he remained—despite the promising signs—anxious and worried. His nervous tension increased when his father complained again in a bitter, disapproving tone, "If your heart really was affectionate, son, it would have set much less store on your position's requirements, which you have used as an excuse, and would have tormented you for allowing your parents to writhe in hunger. I'm amazed at how your mother continues to defend you, rejecting all the charges that were shared with us. She told me, 'Time will show you whether I'm not the one who knows our son best.' I wish she had come with me to see with her own eyes."

Mahgub felt exasperated. He was fed up with the man whose presence had caused his present crisis. He was poised to respond when the doorbell rang to announce a new arrival. Mahgub's heart pounded painfully. Who could it be? Was there something more? The cook opened the door, and then he heard a shrill voice. Outraged, he went to the door of the room and opened it. Then he saw a lady who was brushing the cook out of her way and entering the apartment in a state of intense nervous excitation. She was an elegantly attired lady of aristocratic bearing. He was astonished and alarmed. Then he felt panic-stricken, terrified, and speechless. Seeing him, the woman approached haughtily, her eyes flashing angrily. When she stopped before him, she asked contemptuously, "Are you the person known as Mahgub Abd al-Da'im?"

Mahgub was already predisposed to terror and pessimism. His tormented soul told him that he was the victim of a perfidious plot of which his father was merely one of many lethal weapons. He felt despondent, convinced that his glory hung from a fragile thread. Looking at the woman disapprovingly, he said in a low voice, since he was apprehensive about her loud voice that his father could hear, "Yes, madam, I am."

She scowled angrily, her lips curled disdainfully, and she said harshly, "Come on, show me the room where my husband is secluded with your chaste wife."

This request pierced his heart, splitting it in two, his energy evaporated, and he felt almost oblivious to his surroundings. The woman turned from him toward the bedroom door like a madwoman. She twisted the doorknob but found the door locked. She struck it hard with the palm of her hand, screaming with crazed fury, "Open the door! Open up, man, Mr. Important Minister. Your cover is blown. I saw you enter this brothel with my own eyes. If you don't open the door, I'll break it down."

The young man's despair reached its zenith. He stayed where he was, making no motion, as if he were watching a dreadful calamity that did not concern him and that had no bearing on his destiny. It seemed to be more than he could bear to accept that his glory, for which he had mobilized so much energy and thought and on which he had built so many dreams, could in a minute be annihilated. He sensed his father approaching. He asked, in voice Mahgub had come to hate, "What is it? What is this lady saying?"

The young man, however, did not trouble himself to reply. He seemed not to have heard the question. He no longer noticed him. The woman had not stopped pounding on the door, screaming angrily, "I'm warning you that if you don't open the door voluntarily, I'll have the police open it by force."

Mahgub collected what little energy he retained and approached the lady. In a pleading voice, he said, "Madam . . . ."

231

But she did not allow him to speak. She turned on him and spitefully slapped his face hard, yelling at him, "Don't say a word, you vile pimp."

Mahgub retreated in alarm to where his father was standing, paying no attention to him. Then the door opened, and Qasim Bey Fahmi emerged, closing the door behind him. Mahgub heard the key turn from the inside. The man was trying to put on a brave front, but his discomfort was too profound to hide. He quickly told his wife, "Come outside with me, please."

Crazed with anger, she shouted at him, "Open this door! It must be opened."

In a low voice he replied, "Not so loud, Madam. This isn't becoming."

She yelled sarcastically, "You're going to tell me what's becoming and what's not, Your Excellency the Bey? Do you suppose it's becoming for me to catch you in the bedroom of this insolent pimp's wife? Will you be happy when your son and daughter learn about your praiseworthy conduct?"

"That's enough. Enough. Come with me, and we'll sort through our differences at home."

He tried to take her arm, but she wrested it from his grip contemptuously and shouted, "I'll leave this filthy house, but don't fool yourself into hoping that you can 'sort through' this quarrel. This is the last straw! There'll be no sorting through things after today. My revenge on you will stand for all time as a lesson to libertines."

The woman headed toward the apartment door, with the bey on her heels. They left together.

※

In a hoarse voice, Mahgub muttered, "It's all over."

What an amazing fact it was! Had his monumental struggle miscarried? Wouldn't he ever receive his new salary?

Could fortunes die of cardiac arrest like men?

His father's mournful voice interrupted his reflections. "What does all this mean, son?"

This question might just as well have been gasoline poured on his flaming breast. He turned on his father passionately, his eyes shooting sparks, and said resentfully and rancorously, "It's all over. No more job. No more salary. Let's go beg together."

A stunned, uncertain look appeared in the man's feeble eyes. His bewilderment seemed potentially fatal and his distress pronounced. He could not believe what his eyes had seen and his ears had heard. His pain was agonizing and his anger stifling. Had he not sensed his son's despair and delirium, his own volcano would have erupted. It was not just the job and salary that were finished. His son was too. He had lost his money and his son. If he made it back to his hometown, he would tell his wife, "Don't ask about Mahgub. He's finished. He's nothing but a memory." Then he felt so weak and enervated he was sure he would fall if he did not find a place to sit down. He turned his back on the young man and exited with heavy steps, leaning on his stick, as apt to fall on his face as not.

Mahgub threw himself down on a chair in the sitting room, resting his hand on its arm and leaning his head in the palm of his other hand. The quiet was so pervasive the apartment seemed deserted. Everything was where it belonged, as if his life had not just been turned upside down. Could his rebellious spirit withstand this cascade of erratic fortune? Would he be able to mount a counterattack against this dreadful crisis, brandishing his normal banner: tuzz? What other stratagem could he employ if that didn't work? When suffering conspired against his happiness, how should an egoist, who cared for nothing in the world but himself, react? His only remaining option was death. Damn his luck! How had his glory ended with such insane speed? Wasn't the

233

world crammed full of adventurers on whom it smiled to the end? The sound of light footsteps roused him from his reflections. Raising his heavy head, he saw Ihsan looking at him with a face suffused with the pallor of death. Their eyes met in painful silence, as if each was asking the other: Is this the reward for all our struggle and effort?

Finally, in a weak voice, she asked, "Has everyone left?"

In as weak a voice, he replied, "Yes, as you see."

After hesitating for a moment, she asked, "What will become of us?"

How could he know? All the same, he shook his head and his left hand started to tug at his eyebrow. He said, "I can't predict the future. Anything may happen, but it doesn't look good. Certainly our dreams have evaporated. That's for sure."

A heavy silence followed. Her eyes had a vacant look as she began to recall memories she had accumulated from the past. She remembered her hopes and how they had been dashed, one after the other. Then her breast surged with pain and regret till her eyes were bathed in tears. Mahgub sank into his own reflections once more. He, however, felt no remorse, acknowledged no fault—certainly not—and rejected none of his ideas. He started to wonder whether the morrow would reveal a new life or whether death was all that awaited him. Even so, this time, he gave in and surrendered to despair and depression as a dark cloud swept before his eyes. He did his best to rouse his rebellious spirit, murmuring in a scarcely audible whisper, "tuzz," but this time the interjection—atypically—reflected the despair and submission of his heart.

46

The three pals—Ali Taha, Ahmad Badir, and Ma'mun Radwan—met at the office of the *New Light Journal,* which was published by Ali Taha. Ma'mun Radwan had been spending a lot of time with his two friends as he prepared for his imminent departure. People had been talking recently about nothing besides the major scandal that was on everyone's lips. It was said that Qasim Bey Fahmi's wife had intended to publish a statement in the newspapers that would reveal the reasons for their divorce. It was said that a certain figure had intervened and convinced her to abandon that idea. So the issue was resolved with the minister's resignation. The memo that would have promoted his office manager was withdrawn from consideration by the cabinet and that individual was transferred to Aswan. The scandal was kept out of the newspapers' columns but was no longer a secret to anyone. The three comrades had discussed it with intense regret but had not forgotten their former classmate. They still remembered their relationship with him and the time they had spent together at the university and the hostel.

Of the three, Ali Taha was the most upset, but his pain remained hidden together with its deeper causes. Ahmad Badir said, "Do you all remember our wretched friend's reckless comments? Do you recall his famous 'tuzz'? I always thought it was a bluff or a sarcastic joke—not anything he believed or would implement."

Ma'mun Radwan said in a voice that revealed his distress, "When a person's faith in God is shaken, he becomes an easy prey for every evil."

In spite of his grief and sorrow, Ali Taha smiled and protested, "Allow me to argue against this assertion!"

Ma'mun Radwan amended his claim. "You have your own set of beliefs, even though I think they're inadequate." His large eyes betrayed his smile. Before anyone could comment, he asked, "Do you suppose we'll become sworn enemies in the future?"

Ahmad Badir chortled with laughter and said, "That's for sure. This journal, which you now bless with your hopes for its future, will attack you and accuse you tomorrow of being a stultifying reactionary. And you'll accuse its publisher—your friend—of perverse ideas and atheism and of being a free-thinker. Live and learn!"

The friendly adversaries smiled. Then Ma'mun Radwan declared with confident conviction, "Today's tragedy results from perverse ideas!"

Ali Taha shook his head skeptically and replied, "Many believers are rogues. You don't understand the truth of the matter. Our wretched friend is at one and the same time predator and prey. Don't forget society's role in his offense. The happiness of hundreds of believers assumes the sufferings of millions of others. They are no less at fault than our miserable friend. Our society encourages crime, even though it defends the clique of powerful criminals and destroys the weaker ones. I would like to ask you whether the minister's resignation suffices."

Ma'mun Radwan replied, "Umar ibn al-Khattab wouldn't have hesitated to stone him!"

Ahmad Badir commented sarcastically, "Spare us Umar. Our society can stomach this minister and others like him once he's seasoned with forgetfulness. He'll skulk for a year or two at the Muhammad Ali Club. Future nationalist demonstrations may extricate him from his solitude and carry him heroically back to the ministry. Then he'll return to his previous conduct or play some new role. Live and learn."

Ma'mun Radwan said bitterly, "The fact of the matter is that I think good is spiritual whereas you two see it—or the editor does—as related to a loaf of bread. When bread is distributed fairly, evil is eradicated."

In a rather sharp tone, Ali retorted, "I don't agree with this analysis of the issue. You certainly know I'm a fan of spiritual pleasures. The society we dream of will not be free of evil, because there's nothing good about a society that contains no defect to encourage us to work toward perfection. The society we dream of, however, erases evils we currently consider pre-destined and inevitable."

At this point Ahmad Badir laughed out loud and asked, "Why are the two of you waging your battle now, prematurely?"

The pals smiled, and these friendly adversaries exchanged a knowing look, as if each was wondering what the morrow would bring.

Glossary

Abu al-Ala': see al-Ma'arri.

Amr ibn al-'As (died AD 664): early Arab Muslim conqueror and ruler of Egypt.

Amshir: sixth month (of thirteen) in the Coptic calendar, starting in February and ending in March; also called Meshir.

Any place glory flourishes is fine: half of a line of poetry by al-Mutanabbi.

Bulkeley, Bokla, or Bolkly: tram station and region of Alexandria; once the site of the Egyptain monarchy's summer capital; E.M. Forster's Buckeley: "the heart of Ramleh where the British and other foreigners reside." E.M. Forster, *Alexandria: A History and a Guide* (Garden City: Anchor Books, 1962), p. 181.

By night when it descends: Qur'an, Chapter of *al-Layl* (The Night) 92:1.

By the heavens and by the night star: Qur'an, Chapter of *al-Tariq* (The Night Star) 86:1.

Constitutions of 1923 and 1930: The 1923 Constitution
marked the emergence of Egypt from the British pro-
tectorate. It was abolished by Ismail Sidqi in 1930 and
another, which strengthened the monarchy, was drafted.
The 1923 Constitution was restored in 1935.

cuckold's horns: In various cultures, as in English folklore, it is
thought that a man whose spouse is unfaithful to him
acquires one horn, a pair of horns, or a set of antlers.

cupping: bleeding a patient for medicinal purposes by application
to scarified skin of a cupping-glass.

dhikr: ritual Sufi remembrance of God often involving motion
and music.

ful, ful midammis: a stewed bean dish that is a staple of the
Egyptian diet.

gallabiya: Egyptian ankle-length tunic.

Hanbali: one of the more conservative and puritanical of the
Sunni approaches to law and theology.

*I don't worship what you worship. . . . Nor do we worship what
you worship. You have your religion and I have mine*: Qur'an,
Chapter of *al-Kafirun* (The Unbelievers), 109:2, 4–5,
and 6.

Lalande, André (1867–1963): author of *Vocabulaire technique et
critique de la philosophie* (many editions).

al-Ma'arri, Abu al-Ala' (973–1058): famed Arab poet and author
known for his daring and possibly heretical thought, personal asceticism, and elaborately elegant literary style.

Mach, Ernst (1838–1916): Austrian physicist and philosopher.

Magdeleine, possibly *Marie-Magdeleine*: the popular oratorio
(premiere 1873) by Jules Massenet; or alternatively:
Mary Magdalene, a play in three acts, by Maurice
Maeterlinck; tr. by Alexander Teixera de Mattos (New
York: Dodd, Mead and company, [1910] title page 1911).

mahdi: a messiah-like figure in Islam, especially for Shi'i
    Twelvers, who await the return of the Expected
    Twelfth Imam.
Merneptah: Egyptian pharaoh who ruled from approximately
    1213–1203 BC; his stela referred to ancient Israel as
    'laid waste.'
millieme: in Egyptian currency one tenth of a piaster and thus
    one thousandth of an Egyptian pound (from *millième*).
mish: Egyptian farm cheese, which is soft and easy to spread.
    It is created by an ancient process that involves pickling
    karish cheese, which is itself a low-fat, firm Egyptian
    cheese made from skim milk.
Muhammad Ali Street: Cairo thoroughfare famed for music shops.
al-Mutanabbi (d. AD 965): famous Arab poet.
No wound hurts a dead man: half of a line of poetry by al-
    Mutanabbi.
Ostwald, Wilhelm (1853–1932): Latvian-born pioneer in physical
    chemistry; Nobel laureate for chemistry in 1909.
The Sorrows of Young Werther: landmark novel (1774) by Johann
    Wolfgang von Goethe.
tuzz: a contemptuous interjection.
Umar ibn Abi Rabi'a (AD 644–ca. 712): Arab poet famous for
    love poetry and his romances.
umm: Arabic for 'mother,' or 'mother of,' as in Umm Ihsan and
    Umm Tahiya; a common way to refer to a woman using
    her child's name.
University: from 1908 to 1925 called the Egyptian University,
    then King Fouad University until the 1950s, and now
    Cairo University.
Wafd Party: major liberal, nationalist Egyptian political party
    dating back to Saad Zaghlul and the end of the First
    World War.

Young Egypt: a pro-Fascist political party, founded by Ahmad Husayn in 1933, with a youth wing, the Green Shirts; it evolved with time, changing its name and ideology.

zakat: the duty of a Muslim to purify wealth by assisting certain categories of the disadvantaged.

Translator's Acknowledgments

Since the publication of my translation of *The Cairo Trilogy*, both its executive editor and Naguib Mahfouz have died. I have inevitably thought frequently of them while translating this novel. I wish to thank my friend Fadhil al-Azzawi for help with the poetry by al-Mutanabbi. And, as always, thank you, Sarah, Franya, and Kip Hutchins.

Modern Arabic Literature
from the American University in Cairo Press

Ibrahim Abdel Meguid *Birds of Amber • Distant Train*
No One Sleeps in Alexandria • The Other Place
Yahya Taher Abdullah *The Collar and the Bracelet*
The Mountain of Green Tea
Leila Abouzeid *The Last Chapter*
Hamdi Abu Golayyel *Thieves in Retirement*
Yusuf Abu Rayya *Wedding Night*
Ahmed Alaidy *Being Abbas el Abd*
Idris Ali *Dongola: A Novel of Nubia • Poor*
Ibrahim Aslan *The Heron • Nile Sparrows*
Alaa Al Aswany *Chicago • Friendly Fire • The Yacoubian Building*
Fadhil al-Azzawi *Cell Block Five • The Last of the Angels*
Hala El Badry *A Certain Woman • Muntaha*
Salwa Bakr *The Golden Chariot • The Man from Bashmour*
The Wiles of Men
Halim Barakat *The Crane*
Hoda Barakat *Disciples of Passion • The Tiller of Waters*
Mourid Barghouti *I Saw Ramallah*
Mohamed El-Bisatie *Clamor of the Lake • Houses Behind the Trees • Hunger*
A Last Glass of Tea • Over the Bridge
Mansoura Ez Eldin *Maryam's Maze*
Ibrahim Farghali *The Smiles of the Saints*
Hamdy el-Gazzar *Black Magic*
Tawfiq al-Hakim *The Essential Tawfiq al-Hakim*
Abdelilah Hamdouchi *The Final Bet*
Fathy Ghanem *The Man Who Lost His Shadow*
Randa Ghazy *Dreaming of Palestine*
Gamal al-Ghitani *Pyramid Texts • Zayni Barakat*
Yahya Hakki *The Lamp of Umm Hashim*
Bensalem Himmich *The Polymath • The Theocrat*
Taha Hussein *The Days • A Man of Letters • The Sufferers*
Sonallah Ibrahim *Cairo: From Edge to Edge • The Committee • Zaat*
Yusuf Idris *City of Love and Ashes*
Denys Johnson-Davies *The AUC Press Book of Modern Arabic Literature*
Under the Naked Sky: Short Stories from the Arab World

Said al-Kafrawi *The Hill of Gypsies*
Sahar Khalifeh *The End of Spring*
The Image, the Icon, and the Covenant • *The Inheritance*
Edwar al-Kharrat *Rama and the Dragon* • *Stones of Bobello*
Betool Khedairi *Absent*
Mohammed Khudayyir *Basrayatha: Portrait of a City*
Ibrahim al-Koni *Anubis* • *Gold Dust*
Naguib Mahfouz *Adrift on the Nile* • *Akhenaten: Dweller in Truth*
Arabian Nights and Days • *Autumn Quail* • *The Beggar*
The Beginning and the End • *Cairo Modern*
The Cairo Trilogy: Palace Walk, Palace of Desire, Sugar Street
Children of the Alley • *The Day the Leader Was Killed*
The Dreams • *Dreams of Departure* • *Echoes of an Autobiography*
The Harafish • *The Journey of Ibn Fattouma*
Karnak Café • *Khufu's Wisdom* • *Life's Wisdom* • *Midaq Alley* • *Miramar*
Mirrors • *Morning and Evening Talk* • *Naguib Mahfouz at Sidi Gaber*
Respected Sir • *Rhadopis of Nubia* • *The Search*
The Seventh Heaven • *Thebes at War* • *The Thief and the Dogs*
The Time and the Place • *Voices from the Other World* • *Wedding Song*
Mohamed Makhzangi *Memories of a Meltdown*
Alia Mamdouh *Naphtalene* • *The Loved Ones*
Selim Matar *The Woman of the Flask*
Ibrahim al-Mazini *Ten Again*
Yousef Al-Mohaimeed *Wolves of the Crescent Moon*
Ahlam Mosteghanemi *Chaos of the Senses* • *Memory in the Flesh*
Buthaina Al Nasiri *Final Night*
Ibrahim Nasrallah *Inside the Night*
Haggag Hassan Oddoul *Nights of Musk*
Abd al-Hakim Qasim *Rites of Assent*
Somaya Ramadan *Leaves of Narcissus*
Lenin El-Ramly *In Plain Arabic*
Ghada Samman *The Night of the First Billion*
Rafik Schami *Damascus Nights*
Khairy Shalaby *The Lodging House*
Miral al-Tahawy *Blue Aubergine* • *The Tent*
Bahaa Taher *Love in Exile*
Fuad al-Takarli *The Long Way Back*
Latifa al-Zayyat *The Open Door*